The Lawless Breed

When Wesley Sumner is released from prison, he and cellmate Corey Madison go in search of work as ranch hands. But their new-found freedom is short-lived when they are arrested for a crime they did not commit. And when Corey dies after a savage beating from their captors, Sumner vows revenge. However, his plans are thwarted when he learns that the two deputies who beat Corey have lost their jobs and are now themselves on the run from the law. And so begins a long hard journey, fraught with danger, as slowly but surely Sumner tracks down his friend's killers.

The Lawless Breed

Ralph Hayes

A Black Horse Western

ROBERT HALE

© Ralph Hayes 2017
First published in Great Britain 2017

ISBN 978-0-7198-2163-9

The Crowood Press
The Stable Block
Crowood Lane
Ramsbury
Marlborough
Wiltshire SN8 2HR

www.bhwesterns.com

Robert Hale is an imprint
of The Crowood Press

The right of Ralph Hayes to be identified as
author of this work has been asserted by him
in accordance with the Copyright, Designs and
Patents Act 1988

Typeset by
Derek Doyle & Associates, Shaw Heath
Printed and bound in Great Britain by
CPI Group (UK) Ltd, Croydon, CR0 4YY

CHAPTER ONE

A faint but definite stench of urine and dried sweat hung in the iron-barred cell like a perpetual reminder of grim reality. Age-old graffiti marred the gray walls, and rat droppings decorated the floor in a dark corner where a hole in the concrete served for a toilet.

On one wall, reclining on a lower bunk, Wesley Sumner turned a page of the book he was reading about the Mexican War. He had not known how to read or write when he entered this Texas facility several years ago, but had arduously taught himself until now; his skill in those areas was admirable to other inmates. Sumner looked up from the book now as he heard footsteps approaching his cell. In a moment, a husky guard stood outside the bars with a young inmate.

'Wake up, Sumner. You got a visitor.'

A key clanged in the cell door and the two men entered. Sumner threw his book aside and sat up on his bunk.

'I was told I'd be alone for these last days,' he said in a rather deep voice. He was a tall, slim young man in his early twenties, with dark hair and eyes and a square,

5

handsome face. His good looks had got him in trouble on his arrival at the prison, but after a deadly fight with another inmate that earned him a thick scar on his chest that he still bore, the other men in his cell block left him alone.

'This here is Corey Madison,' the burly guard said gruffly. 'He gets out in a couple days, just ahead of you. His old cell is being hosed down.'

The boy named Corey looked about twelve to Sumner. Reddish hair. The vestiges of freckles. Not as tall as Sumner.

'I hear you're Sumner.' Corey grinned at him. 'Pleasured to meet up with you.'

Sumner stared coldly at him.

'Shut up, Madison,' the guard growled. He looked over at Sumner. 'You behave yourself now, Sumner. He'll be gone Thursday. He's just a wet-behind-the-ears kid. Put up with him.' He gave Sumner a hard grin. 'We'd appreciate it.'

Sumner looked Corey over with disdain. 'They said I'd finish it out alone.' Quietly. To himself.

The guard gave him a sour look. 'Behave.' Then he turned and left the cell, the door clanging behind him.

Sumner sighed. 'When you get into that upper bunk, try not to bring the whole thing down on me.'

The boy Corey was grinning again. 'I'll turn eighteen not long after I blow this joint. I can buy my own booze then.'

'You're only seventeen?' Sumner said acidly. 'You're starling young, boy.'

'I heard you come in here at the same age,' Corey offered. He had leaned against the opposite wall. 'What are you in for?'

Sumner looked up at him soberly. 'Murder.'

A silence fell into the small room that seemed to erect a thick wall between them. After a long moment Corey said in a subdued tone, 'Oh.'

Sumner lay back down and propped his head on two pillows, then pulled one out and threw it to Corey. 'This one is yours. You ought to make up your bed.'

Corey nodded, and climbed up over Sumner. Sumner could feel him moving around up above for a few minutes, then it was quiet up there. It was rather early in the evening but Sumner hoped the kid went to sleep. In a few more minutes, though, Corey's voice came to him from the upper bunk.

'I got in a saloon fight,' his high voice came to Sumner. 'My sister Janie tries to keep me at home, but I don't pay much attention. We live together, our folks bought it in that last influenza epidemic. You might have heard. Anyway, this cowpoke started on me, and we got into it. They didn't arrest him. Just me. I got thirty days, and the local jail was full. So here I am.'

'You've been here thirty days?' Sumner said.

'You wouldn't have seen me. They wouldn't let me mix.'

'So you knocked a cowboy down.' Smiling now in the semi-dark.

'I think I broke his nose. I didn't mean to.'

Sumner's smile widened slightly. 'Sounds like you got grit, kid.'

'I don't like to be hoorawed.' A moment of silence. 'You don't seem like a killer.'

Sumner's face went somber. 'It's not courtesy to yaw

7

over another man's sentence, boy.'

Up on the other bunk, Corey's face flushed slightly. 'Sorry.'

Another stony silence. But then, after a few minutes, Sumner broke it. 'I was just sixteen. Living with my aunt. Like you, I had no parents. One day, three men rode up to our cabin. We offered them coffee and biscuits. When they were finished, they beat me so badly I couldn't stand up. Then they tied me up and raped my aunt. All of them. They made me watch. Then they slit her throat. They were going to kill me too, but one of them said it was better this way. Then he laughed. And they laughed.'

When he paused for a moment, Corey thought he had never heard such a heavy silence.

'It took me almost twenty-four hours to get loose from the ropes. Then I buried my aunt out in back of the cabin. And I made a pledge to her. I told her I'd find those men. If it took all my life.'

'And you did find them,' Corey suggested.

'It took over a year. But I found two of them in a saloon. I had taught myself to shoot by then. It wasn't a draw-down. I just executed them. The way you would step on a snake. I caught up with the last man on a ranch when he was out mending fence. I shot him and his mount. But that didn't save me. The law found me buying groceries in a general store. I gave up without a fight.'

'I was right,' Corey's voice came in the darkness. 'You ain't no killer.'

'I'm being released on Saturday. Because of good behavior,' Sumner finished. 'They just turn you loose. They don't even give you a horse. Most inmates have someone meeting them.'

'But you don't,' Corey guessed.

'I don't know anybody,' Sumner said. 'But I like it that way.'

'They're setting me loose two days ahead of you,' Corey said. 'We could almost have gone together.'

'I'm fine with alone,' Sumner told him.

Corey hesitated. 'Sure. Of course.'

'Incidentally, kid.'

'Yeah?'

'You're wrong about me.'

'What do you mean, Sumner?'

'I think I am a killer. If the situation demands it.' Very quietly.

'What kind of "situation"?'

Sumner folded his hands behind his head, on his thin pillow. 'I don't have an occupation. I never had time to learn one. When I first came in here I met an inmate that had been a bounty hunter. He always went after men who were wanted dead or alive. And he never took them in for trial.'

'He killed all of them?'

'He only went after killers. He felt no remorse about it. I'd feel the same way. After what I've seen.'

'How did he end up here?'

'Some gambler back-shot his best friend, and he vowed he would take him down the same way. He found the gambler, put a bullet in his back, and was arrested for murder by a sheriff who hated bounty hunters.'

'But he isn't here now?'

'He broke out a year ago, and they shot him dead in a marsh just a mile from here.'

9

This time the silence was deafening.

'And you'd like to do that for a living?' Corey pursued.

Sumner shrugged in the dark. 'I doubt they'd hire me for a town marshal.' He grinned to himself.

Corey grinned, too. 'I see what you mean. They'd figure you for the lawless breed. Because of this.'

Sumner grunted. 'It puts you in a pigeon hole that's hard to crawl out of.'

After a moment, Corey responded. 'I don't give that sort of thinking credence. You'll do to tie to, Sumner.'

Sumner looked up toward the upper bunk. 'Go to sleep, kid. We've got another day in this hellhole tomorrow.'

'Good night, Sumner,' his young voice came from above.

The next day Sumner and Corey Madison were taken to the mess hall together, shared a bowl in the washroom, and visited the big prison yard together for their daily airing. A couple hundred of other prisoners milled about in the gravel yard with its high concrete walls all around. Watch towers stood ominously at each corner of the walls, with men holding rifles at ready. Each tower also had an impressive-looking Gatling gun aimed at the center of the yard.

'I hate this place,' Corey complained to Sumner as they stood in the spring sun together, enjoying the way it felt on their backs.

'How would you like it for a few years?' Sumner suggested acidly.

'I couldn't do it,' Corey said glumly, his red hair glinting in the sun. Sumner thought he looked particularly young out here in the daylight. 'I'd probably try an escape, like that fellow you told me about. And end up dead in a mucky swamp.'

'You adjust,' Sumner said, remembering. 'You hunker down, and you say it won't beat you. And you find out you can survive.'

'I still don't see how you did it,' Corey admitted. He stretched his arms out and took in a big lungful of fresh air. 'I need to be in the open.'

Sumner smiled slightly. 'Then you better stay out of trouble, kid,' he said.

At that moment, a large bald inmate walked over to Sumner and addressed him. 'Hey, Sumner. I hear you're out of here soon.'

'I'll be gone Saturday,' Sumner told him. 'Oh. This is Corey. They put him in with me. He's out tomorrow.'

The big fellow looked Corey over. 'Are you even out of grade school?'

Corey's face flushed. 'I'm almost eighteen!'

The newcomer laughed softly, then turned back to Sumner. 'I got something to ask you, Sumner.' He glanced again at Corey.

Sumner nodded, and guided him off to one side. 'You stay put, Corey.'

Corey frowned but nodded.

A few feet distant from Corey, the other inmate handed Sumner an envelope. 'Would you mail this for me when you get outside? I'm not sure my letters are getting to my wife. If she don't hear from me, she might just take off and I'll never see her again.'

Sumner nodded. 'Of course. Unless they find it on me.'

11

'Much obliged. You're the only one I'd trust it with.'

Sumner stuffed it into a pocket of his prison shirt. He started to make a parting comment to the other man when he heard Corey's voice behind him.

'Hell, no! Get to hell away from me!'

Sumner turned to look, and saw that Corey had been accosted by a large Mestizo who had given Sumner trouble on his arrival years ago.

'Hey, come on, little *putito*. You meet me in the C Block washroom tonight at grub time, *sí*? We have us a little fiesta. You know, party!' He reached out and touched Corey's shoulder.

Corey threw the hand off him, scowling. 'I told you. Keep away from me, you goddamn greaser!'

The crooked grin on the Mexican's face slid into a fierce scowl, and in the next moment, a short-blade knife appeared magically in his hand.

'You can cooperate, or I will find you alone and cut your liver out and have it for *cena*, my evening meal.' In a menacing tone.

Sumner walked over to them. 'Are you up to your old habits again, Gomez?'

Gomez cast a brittle look on him. 'Oh, you. Keep out of this, Sumner. He is mine, or he is *muerte*.'

'If he's yours, you are *muerte*,' Sumner said in a hard voice. A few other inmates had gathered around quietly. The whole prison knew that Sumner was in for multiple murder, and that he had made Gomez back off once before, in a knife fight.

Sumner's friend who had given him the letter now stepped up beside him. He was a big, muscular fellow with a scar across his lower face. 'That goes for me, too,' he growled ominously at Gomez.

Gomez looked from Sumner to the big man. 'So that is the way it is, Walcott.'

'That's the way,' Walcott answered grimly.

Gomez hesitated, then put the knife away. He turned to Sumner fiercely. 'You are *afortunado*, Sumner. That you leave this week.'

'That's the way I look at it,' Sumner retorted.

Gomez moved off then with a couple of Mexican cohorts. When they were gone, Walcott grinned at Corey. 'You should have come with a nursemaid, kid.'

Corey frowned through his relief. 'I can take care of myself.'

'Sure,' Walcott said. 'And that moon that comes up tonight is made of Swiss cheese.'

Corey looked at the ground, frowning. 'That saucy line don't impress me, mister.'

Walcott chuckled. 'It's good you're getting out of here tomorrow, kid. You wouldn't last a month here.' He turned to Sumner. 'Don't forget that letter, Sumner. And thanks.'

'My pleasure,' Sumner told him. He waited until Walcott was gone, and turned to Corey. 'You got clabber for brains, boy?'

Corey looked hurt. 'Now you're on me?'

'You have one day left. When somebody like Gomez threatens you in those circumstances, you work him. Appease him. Put him off. He probably doesn't even know you're leaving. Fake him off his feet.'

'You didn't. I heard all about it.'

'I had years ahead of me. Positions had to be taken.' A whistle had blown, and other inmates were filing back

13

inside. 'You stick to me like glue till you're released tomorrow. Then if I'm lucky I won't ever see you again.'

'That ain't very friendly.'

'Hey, I saved your butt once already this morning. What the hell do you want for one day?' He gave the youngster a wry smile. 'Come on, kid. We're due back at the cage.'

Corey sighed. 'It's like a goddamn zoo,' he uttered bitterly.

The next twenty-four hours passed uneventfully, because of Sumner's defence of Corey in the yard, and Corey said goodbye to Sumner in their cell.

'You be careful out there now,' Sumner advised him. 'No more saloon brawls for a while. Just go home and take care of your sister.'

Corey held a bag of personal items under his arm. He stood beside Sumner's bunk awkwardly. 'Well. I hope we meet up outside some time, Sumner,' he said quietly.

'Oh, I doubt that,' Sumner replied, sitting on the edge of his bunk.

'It's been an honor bunking with you.'

Sumner looked up at him, marveling at his youth and innocence. Actually, there were barely six years' difference in their ages. But Sumner had had the experience and trauma of two decades thrust into less than one.

'I appreciate that, Corey. Watch out for the law now.' A tired smile.

A moment later, a guard came and got Corey and he was released and gone. Now the cell seemed very empty without him, and Sumner felt a little lonely for the first time in years. But his time was very short, and Saturday came storming at him before he really wanted it to be there. He was not prepared for release, he suddenly realized. He had not had a life when he came there, so there was nothing to go back to now. It was a little unsettling. He knew what each day brought him while he was here. After release, he had no idea. That thing he had discussed with Corey about taking up hunting other men for the bounties on their heads was just misguided expectation. He had almost no skill with a gun. He didn't even own one. He didn't know a Colt from an Enfield.

There was a very brief meeting with the warden that Saturday, who bored him with a prescribed lecture on recidivism. It ended with the warden's observation that he fully expected to see Sumner back there in the near future. Sumner carefully held his tongue, and a half hour later, was escorted to the big front gate by a guard.

'See you soon, Sumner.' The fellow grinned.

Then Sumner walked out of the gate into a bright sunny day. He stretched his arms out to receive the luxury of spring, and took a deep breath in. Then he glanced to his left and saw Corey Madison sitting against the wall, grinning at him.

'What the hell!' Sumner exclaimed.

'Hi, Sumner.' Corey rose to his feet, looking gangly in his home clothes: a checked shirt under a plain vest, and denim trousers.

Sumner looked past him and saw two roan stallions, both saddled. He walked over to Corey and the boy came and lightly embraced him, making Sumner frown. He ignored the gesture and looked Corey over.

'You look somehow more mature in those clothes.'

'They used to belong to my daddy. Before he died. My sister found them for me. Look. I got us mounts.'

Sumner glanced at the horses again. 'How long have you been out here?'

'Oh, I come last night. I didn't want to miss you.'

'Good God, kid. You didn't have to do that. A stage comes past here this afternoon, and I have enough cash to get on it.'

Corey looked Sumner over, too. He was wearing the work clothes he had come there in years ago. The shirt looked a little tight on him. Corey assessed the tall, athletic look of Sumner. The broad shoulders, the muscular frame.

'Where would you take a stage to?' Corey asked him soberly.

'I didn't have that worked out yet,' Sumner admitted.

'Well. My sister – that's Janie – thought you ought to come home with me. Till you get things figured out.'

Sumner smiled. 'Oh no,' he protested. 'I wouldn't think of it. I've always preferred to be on my own, kid. Must wait here for that stagecoach. It will take me somewhere.'

Corey looked frustrated. 'Look, Sumner. This ain't just between you and me. If I don't show up with you this afternoon, Jane will lay into me something fierce. Do you want to see that happen to your old cellmate on his first weekend out from behind them bars? I'd be mighty pleasured if you'd spare me that.'

That prompted a light chuckle in Sumner's throat. He cast a slow look on that earnest, freckled face and decided he liked the boy.

'Now this sister. Jane, you call her? She isn't going to keep a gun in her apron, is she? Because of who I am?'

Corey grinned broadly. 'She might pick up a frying

pan, though. But I reckon it would be me she'd go after. You'll come then? Our farm is only two hours' ride south. We can be there in early afternoon.'

Sumner sighed. 'OK, kid. I'll ride there with you. But then I'll be moving on. I might keep the horse and pay you for it later if that's OK.'

'Don't pay that no mind,' Corey told him. 'Janie's got a little chestnut mare she keeps for her buggy. Shall we ride?'

Sumner clapped him on the shoulder. 'Let's get away from this place,' he agreed.

A few minutes later, they were headed south. Sumner's stallion shied on him when he first climbed aboard, but then became accustomed to his smell and feel. They rode leisurely through arid Texas back country on that early spring day, surrounded by prickly pear and jumping cholla, and passing under plane and mesquite trees. At one point they saw a small herd of cattle bunched up against a low butte, chewing their cud into the wind, and Corey identified the ranch and indicated they were just five miles from the farm.

They were riding side by side. 'How long have your parents been gone?' Sumner asked him, tuning in his saddle.

'Almost three years,' Corey said, staring into the distance. 'It sure changed our lives. We inherited the farm jointly but we didn't know much about working it. Of course, Jane knew how to keep house. But I had no idea really how to manage a farm. She didn't, either. We grow some corn. And there's the swine and chickens to look after. And the milk cow.'

'That doesn't seem enough to keep you going,'

Sumner suggested.

'Oh, Janie does laundry for a rancher. And a different one gives me odd jobs to perform. We get along. But I doubt anybody hereabouts will hire me now.'

'You never know. Some men are willing to let the past lie where it is.'

At that moment a small farm house came into view, as they crested a low rise of ground. 'Well, here we are!' Corey announced.

They rode up into the dirt yard and Sumner looked the place over. The house looked well kept, with ivy growing on one side of a small porch. Chickens ran free around the yard, and Sumner could see a low barn behind the house, with a pigsty beside it. An open buggy sat off to one side of the porch.

'She keeps that for town,' Corey said, seeing Sumner eyeing it. 'Blaneyville is only five miles off. We get our supplies there.'

'That's where you got into trouble?' Sumner said.

They both dismounted. 'There's a saloon there. A lot of cowboys come there. They don't mean no harm.'

'I reckon you ought to try to get along with them for a while now.' Sumner grinned at him.

They swaddled their reins over a short hitching post near the porch. Corey was about to respond to Sumner when a girl emerged from the house and stood facing them on the porch.

'Oh, there you are!' her melodious voice came to them. 'I've been watching for most of an hour!'

Sumner released his hold on his reins and just stared for a long moment. He hadn't seen a young woman for several years, and this one took his breath away. Jane

Madison was obviously not much older than Corey and she was nice to look at. Her hair wasn't as reddish as her brother's, more of a subdued auburn, and it hung straight to her shoulders. She had bright blue eyes and a strong chin and a perfectly chiseled face, with high cheek bones. Her figure, in a blue gingham dress, was slim and curvaceous.

'Good Jesus,' Sumner muttered.

'We're back, sis!' Corey was calling out. 'I got him to come!'

Corey led Sumner up onto the porch, where Sumner got an even better look at Jane. She was probably, he thought, the prettiest girl he had ever met.

'Jane, this is my friend Sumner,' Corey announced happily. He turned to Sumner. 'I told her all about you,' he added confidentially.

Jane was staring at Sumner, appraising his good looks. She extended her hand to him, as a man would. 'Pleasured, Sumner. I'm Jane Madison.'

He liked the way she seemed to take charge. 'The pleasure is mine, believe me.'

Her face colored slightly. 'So you and Corey spent some time together. Behind bars.'

He wasn't sure if there was an indictment in the last words. 'Well. A few days. I enjoyed his company. He made the time go fast.'

She finally smiled at him. She acted just a little scared, and she was wondering if she had made the right decision in suggesting Corey bring him home. 'He can't quit talking about you.'

'Janie!' Corey frowned at her.

'We wanted to give you a place to sleep while you

decide what you're doing,' she told Sumner.

'I'm very much obliged, ma'am,' Sumner told her. 'This made today a whole lot better.'

She smiled nicely. 'We're glad to help.'

'Come on, everybody,' Corey said. 'Let's get inside, I'm so thirsty I could drink swamp water from my saddle bag! I'll unsaddle the horses later.'

'I have some stew on the stove,' Jane told them.

It was less than an hour later when they were all sitting at a table in the centre of a dining room just off the parlour. It was a comfortable-looking house, and Jane took good care of it. Jane had served them her beef stew with thick slices of bread, and Sumner thought how much better it was than prison grub. When they were all about finished, Jane turned to Sumner. She had been eyeing him surreptitiously throughout the meal.

'Corey says you had to kill some men.'

The abruptness of it surprised Sumner. Corey saw the look on Sumner's face and scowled silently at his sister.

Sumner picked up a chunk of homemade bread. 'Yes, ma'am.'

Her blue eyes were somber. 'I'm sorry to hear that.'

That seems like a hundred years ago, ma'am.'

'Call me Jane.'

'All right. Jane.'

'But you gave them a chance to defend themselves, of course?'

Sumner set his fork down. 'No, Jane. I just shot them down. No warning. No notice. But I did identify myself. I wanted them to know who was sending them to their Maker.'

Jane looked even more somber. 'I see.'

'For God's sake, Jane,' Corey protested. 'These were cold-blooded killers. Sumner wanted justice. Not a shooting medal.'

'It's all right, Corey,' Sumner said quietly.

'But doesn't that make you a cold-blooded killer?' Jane pursued, ignoring her brother.

'Goddamn it, Jane!'

Sumner regarded her narrowly. 'That's what the law said,' he said evenly. 'Some nights at three in the morning, that's what I think.'

Jane looked down at her plate.

'If this makes a difference to you, I'll ride out today,' Sumner told her. 'I wouldn't want to cause you any trouble.'

'Sumner is no killer!' Corey spat at her. 'If he rides out, so do I!'

Jane looked over at him, and put a hand on his. 'I wouldn't ask him to leave,' she said.

'Jane,' Sumner addressed her. 'I don't know if what I did was right. But I was a hard case then. There was a fire in my belly to avenge my aunt's rape and murder. I didn't care much how it happened. Just as long as it got done. And I was not quite Corey's age here when it all happened.'

'You could have gone to the law,' Jane suggested.

Corey rose from his chair and threw a napkin on the table. 'I've had enough of this! I'm going to bed the horses down. You want to come, Sumner?'

Sumner hesitated. 'No. I'll sit with your sister.'

'Suit yourself,' Corey grumbled. Then he was gone. They heard him slam the screen door behind him.

'You'll have to excuse Corey,' Jane said. 'We've had

these fights ever since we were three.'

'He's a good kid,' Sumner said. 'He handled himself well while he was there. He has grit.'

'He gets his temper from his daddy.' Jane smiled. She looked into his dark eyes. 'So you were an orphan for a while. Like us.'

Sumner nodded. 'My aunt treated me like a son. I miss her.' He stared across the room, remembering.

'I can see you have deep feelings,' she offered.

He focused on her. Without trying, she whetted a man's appetite. With every move. Every gesture. 'Maybe this is too personal. But why isn't a girl that looks like you married yet?'

She blushed slightly. She looked away for a moment. 'There was a young man. About a year ago. I liked him. He talked some of marriage. But then he hired on to do some cattle droving and we never saw him again.'

'He obviously doesn't know what he missed,' Sumner observed.

There was a long silence. Outside, one of the horses whinnied softly out by the barn.

'I don't think you're a killer, Sumner,' Jane finally said.

Sumner looked into those pretty eyes. 'I honestly don't know what I am, Jane. I haven't had a chance to find out. I only know I can survive in prison. With a little luck.'

'I'm sorry. For everything you've been through.'

'I earned the last part,' he said. 'Now I have to figure out what the rest of it is going to be like.'

'What would you like to do?'

He shrugged. 'Ranch hand. When I was younger, I

always thought I'd like to drive a stagecoach. Or ride shotgun.'

'There are ranches around here.'

'I think Corey is right about that. They probably all know where we've been. They might not care much about Corey. But they would shy away from me something fierce, I reckon.'

At that moment Corey came back through the house and stood beside the dining table. Looking a bit sheepish. 'The horses are eating. Did I make a fool of myself?'

'Of course not,' Jane told him. 'And everything is just fine here. I'm beginning to. . .' She paused. 'Like your friend.'

Corey smiled his freckled smile. Sumner was regarding Jane hungrily, and hoped it didn't show. He felt a little guilty.

'The feeling is mutual,' he said quietly. Their eyes met, and Jane felt a little breathless.

Corey took his chair at the table again, smiling at their mutual reaction. He clasped his hands on the table. 'I didn't mention this to either of you. But I talked to a local cowpoke just before I went and got Sumner. He says there's a rancher over in the Territory that's hiring. I thought me and Sumner could ride over there.'

'The Indian Territory?' Jane exclaimed. 'Why, that's nothing but rogue redskins and outlaws! That's a dangerous place, Corey. Anyway, you can't leave me here all alone to run this farm.'

'Sumner might find a job there. But I wouldn't be asking. I'd try to get a letter of recommendation for one of the ranches hereabouts. Jenkins says the boss there just might do that. Then I could go to work for one of these ranches nearby. Jenkins already put a good word in for me over there.'

'That might work,' Sumner said. 'But you could just apply here first. Somebody might say yes.'

'And if they all say no, it would be over,' Corey argued.

'That's a chance you'd have to take,' Sumner said.

'I'll try the other way,' Corey said resolutely. 'And I'd like you to ride with me, Sumner. You ain't got nothing better to do. Have you?'

Sumner sat there thinking. Jane was right. A kid like Corey could get into trouble fast in the Territory. He sighed. 'No. I have nothing better to do.'

'Then we'll ride out tomorrow!' Corey beamed.

Jane looked from his face to the sober one of Sumner. Since her brother's mind was made up, she was glad Sumner was going, too. She sighed more heavily than Sumner had.

'I'll make up some grub to take with you,' she said softly.

CHAPTER TWO

It was a two days' ride to the Prescott ranch over in the Indian Territory. Sumner and Corey camped out on the trail overnight together, and talked about their past, and got to know each other better. Sumner was growing quite fond of the young man, and hoped he obtained a good recommendation from Hank Prescott, who had spoken previously with Corey's friend from Blaneyville.

On the afternoon of the second day they reached the Prescott ranch. They rode for an hour on Prescott property before reaching the ranch house.

It was a big, sprawling place surrounded by plane trees. They were met on a wide veranda by a foreman, who looked them over with disdain.

'What can we do for you, boys?'

'We're here to see Mr Prescott,' Corey spoke up. 'I'm Corey Madison and this here is Wesley Sumner.'

The foreman's face changed. 'Oh. You two. He knows you're coming. Come on in.'

He led them into a grand foyer decorated with potted palms and tapestries. They could have been in a Kansas

City mansion. Corey and Sumner exchanged a look of surprise.

'You can wait for him in here,' the slim foreman told them. 'He'll be right with you.' In a sour tone.

He took them into a carpeted room where the walls held bookshelves from wall to floor. The foreman disappeared, and Corey looked around uncomfortably. 'Maybe this was a bad idea.'

Sumner smiled. 'Just relax, kid. This doesn't make him God almighty. He's probably a good old boy.'

He had just finished that thought when Prescott walked into the room. 'Afternoon, boys. I'm Hank Prescott.' He didn't extend his hand to either of them. 'I reckon you're Madison.' Eyeing Corey carefully.

'Yes, sir. And this is Wesley Sumner. My best friend.'

A half smile edged onto Sumner's handsome face. 'My pleasure, Mr Prescott.' He extended his hand. Prescott hesitated just a moment and then took it.

'All right, boys,' Presott said. 'Take some weight off, you two.' He indicated a sofa just behind them.

Sumner and Corey sat side by side on the sofa as Prescott pulled a straight chair over to them. 'Now,' he said with a small sigh. He was a big man with a pot belly and silver in his hair. 'I understand you want to be a ranch hand, Madison.'

'Yes, sir. I prefer to work on the Seger ranch, a few miles from my farm, over near Blaneyville.'

'Yes, Jenkins was here. He spoke highly of you.' He glanced at Sumner. 'Despite your recent experience with the law.'

'That was just a friendly hoorawing that ended up worse than it should. That ain't me, Mr Prescott. You

26

could ask my sister.'

'I'm afraid that would be inconvenient.' Prescott smiled wanly.

Corey swallowed. 'Oh. Sure, I'm sorry, sir.'

'If I understand this correctly, you heard that I'm a good friend of Ezra Seger, and you want me to vouch for your character, just on the word of your friend from Blaneyville.'

Corey hesitated. 'Well. Yes, sir.'

'Why didn't you go directly to Seger? He's a half hour away from you there.'

'Jenkins don't know Seger,' Corey explained. 'But he used to work for you. He thought if you gave me a good word, Seger would hire me. But probably not if I went there directly.'

'I've known the boy for a while now,' Sumner said. 'And I'd be honored to work with him.'

Prescott cast a narrow look on him. 'And you're the cellmate from that Texas prison.'

Sumner eyed him soberly. 'That's right.'

'Well, you'll excuse me, I'm sure, if I don't give that much credence.' Holding Sumner's sober look.

Corey looked flustered. 'Oh, Sumner is all right, Mr Prescott. He's about the best man I ever met.'

Prescott nodded. 'Well, I place a high value on Jenkins's judgment. And I like what I see in front of me. I'd be fine with hiring you here. So I'll send a note back to Seger that I think he should hire you. That should probably do it for you.'

Corey burst into a wide smile. 'Thank you, Mr Prescott. You won't never regret it.'

Prescott nodded and looked over to Sumner. 'It's also

my understanding that you'd like to hire on here, Sumner.'

'That's right, sir,' Sumner answered quietly. 'I have a little experience on a ranch down in southern Texas. And it seems like something that would suit me.'

Prescott sighed heavily. 'We heard about you before you got here. Your past isn't exactly like Madison's.'

Sumner held his gaze. 'No. It isn't.'

'He tracked down murderers!' Corey said quickly. 'He shouldn't never been locked up!'

'I understand,' Prescott answered him. 'If it was up to me I might take you on. But I care what my men think about those they work with. I let them take a vote, and they voted no, Sumner.'

Sumner and Corey just sat there silent for a moment.

'Maybe if I talked to them,' Corey said.

Sumner put a hand on his arm. 'No, Corey. I understand perfectly, Mr Prescott. I think you were very fair. A lot more fair than the system has been to me.'

'I'm sorry,' Prescott told him. 'Maybe another ranch around here. Or try at Seger's place when Madison goes there.'

Sumner rose. 'I'll figure it out. No hard feelings, Mr Prescott.'

Corey rose too. Glumly, Prescott had risen with Sumner.

'I'll get your note ready and meet you out on the stoop,' Prescott said.

A few minutes later, Sumner and Corey were saddled up with Corey's note to Seger stuffed safely into a saddle bag. As they rode out, the foreman who had taken them into the house was standing outside the nearby bunkhouse, and gave Sumner a hard grin as they passed him.

After a two hour ride, with both of them quiet all the way, Sumner stopped them for a late afternoon break beside a shallow stream where a stand of aspens afforded a coot shade. They didn't build a fire, they were just giving the horses a rest. They sat on the ground on the bank of the creek and listened to the soothing gurgle of rippling water at their feet.

'I got you all the way over here, and I'm the only one that got anything from it,' Corey muttered. Poking a stick into the ground.

'I didn't really expect to be hired,' Sumner told him. 'I just came to see you get a new start. Be happy with that, Corey. It's a lucky day for you.'

'I'm not trying to throw mud on nobody, but I think it was that foreman that killed it for you. That don't set well in my craw.'

'I'm telling you, forget it,' Sumner insisted. 'I have.'

'I'll talk to Seger about you,' Corey said. 'Hey, you can stay at our place while we look. Anyway, I think Janie is sweet on you.' He turned and gave Sumner a sly grin.

Sumner met his look. 'I don't think that would work, Corey. I'm going to take Prescott's advice and check out some ranches here in the Territory. Where we camp tonight is where we'll be parting company.'

'Hell,' Corey grumbled. 'How will I know where you end up?'

That question touched Sumner. He clapped Corey on the shoulder. 'I'll write to you. And I might appear on your doorstep one day when you least expect it.'

Corey gave him a half grin. Sumner stood up, and Corey followed suit. 'We better move on,' Sumner said.

'The mounts have had a good drink.'

They got the two roans ready to ride, and were about to saddle up when Sumner heard the approach of riders. He stopped cinching his saddle and stood gazing out across the scrub landscape.

'Two riders,' Corey commented. Unconcerned.

But Sumner was wary. Neither of them was armed. Corey wasn't familiar with guns, and Sumner had stopped carrying one after his triple killing.

The riders were just thirty yards away, and coming up to them.

They reined in just a few yards away.

They both wore badges.

For a moment they just stared at Sumner and Corey. Then the slightly taller one spoke. 'Who the hell are you two?'

Sumner and Corey exchanged a sober look.

'We're just traveling back to Texas,' Sumner replied carefully. 'You boys Territory Marshals?'

They both ignored the question. They dismounted and walked over to the twosome. The one who had spoken to them was Duke Pritchard. He stood at just over six feet, about Sumner's height, and had a scar running across his right eye. He had a broken nose and had the look of a retired boxer. He had a reputation among his kind of having beaten a man to death in Wichita with his bare hands before he had joined the marshal service here in the Territory. He and his partner both wore Colt Army .45 revolvers low on their hips.

'Texas?' the other deputy barked out. 'The great land of cow pucky and buffalo dung?' A harsh grin. His name was Maynard Guthrie and he had come to the Territory a few years back, running from the law in Missouri. Many of his appointed brethren had a similar background. He was slim but wiry with cold blue eyes. He was a sociopath who loved to use the gun he carried on his belly, and had killed his own sister three years ago, in a cabin on the Upper Platte.

Corey was getting impatient. 'What can we do for you, gentlemen? We're trying to get clear of this country as quick as we can.'

The one called Pritchard came up very close to Corey. A new frown on his heavy face. 'So you're in a big hurry to clear out?' he said slowly in a deep growl.

'He didn't mean it that way,' Sumner put in, trying to keep calm in his voice. 'He's got a job waiting for him over in Blaneyville.'

He studied Pritchard's hard face and wished he and Corey were armed. He had become physically tough in prison, but that meant nothing against guns. Guthrie moved over to him. Sumner looked into those vacuous eyes and realized he was dealing with something emotionally less than entirely human.

'What's your name, boy?' In a soft, sibilant voice.

'Sumner. Wesley Sumner. I'm just riding with Corey here.'

'Sumner. Sounds familiar. You're going to Texas, too?'

Sumner shook his head. 'No, I'm not sure where I'm headed.'

The two tough-looking lawmen exchanged a look.

'Looks like you boys is just making it up as you go,' Pritchard suggested. 'Where you been the last twenty-four hours?'

'We just come from the Prescott ranch,' Corey piped

31

up nervously.

'Looking for work there, too?' Guthrie said tartly.

'No, it was just to talk with Mr Prescott,' Corey answered, beginning to act guilty for something he couldn't figure out.

'Is there a Prescott ranch around here?' Pritchard asked Guthrie.

'Never heard of one in these parts,' Guthrie said.

'It's half a day's ride from here,' Corey gushed. 'You can check.'

Pritchard came even closer to Corey, and even walked all the way around him. Then he turned to Guthrie. 'What do you think?'

Guthrie nodded. 'He fits the description.'

Sumner frowned at them. 'What the hell is this?'

Pritchard came over nose to nose with him. His scar glistened in the hard sun. 'Ever hear of the Spencer family?'

'Hell, no,' Sumner replied impatiently.

'What about you?' Guthrie asked Corey, moving closer to him. Corey looked into those opaque eyes and swallowed hard.

'I never heard that name,' he said unconvincingly.

'Well, let me tell you about them,' Pritchard said slowly. He casually drew the Colt at his hip, and held it up level with Corey's face. Guthrie pulled the one off his belly and held it on Sumner.

'Last night,' Pritchard continued, 'while Mr Spencer was gone and their boy was out in the barn, someone come to the house, murdered Rebecca Spencer, and made off with some petty cash in the amount of $140.'

Corey swallowed again. 'I'm real sorry to hear that.'

'Fortunately, the Spencer boy saw the murderer as he run off,' Guthrie continued for his partner. 'And you fit the description of the man he saw.'

'What?' Corey breathed.

'This boy was with me last night!' Sumner said loudly. 'Before we arrived at the Prescott ranch. And he doesn't have any stolen money.'

'Well. Maybe he spent it. And if you're vouching for him, maybe you was there, too. Looks like you're both going down to Fort Sill.'

Now Corey panicked. 'I'm telling you! I never heard of no Spencers! I never been to no Spencer place! We just rode to the Prescott ranch, and was there a while, then we rode on back here. On our way home.'

He was breathless looking into the muzzle of Pritchard's gun.

'Oh, you ain't going to Texas now, boy.' Pritchard grinned. 'You're goddamn murdering scum, and you're going to pay a visit to Judge Hezekiah Gabriel. They call him the Hanging Judge.' A low chuckle.

'Just ride to Prescott with me!' Corey fairly yelled at them.

'What for?' Pritchard said. 'He wasn't with you last night, was he?'

'No, but he can vouch for this boy's character,' Sumner intervened. 'He's never shot anybody in his life.'

'What about your friend?' Guthrie purred.

'That was justified!' Corey blurted out. 'He told me all about it when we was locked up together!'

As soon as he said it, he realized his mistake. He glanced at Sumner, who was regarding him seriously. Guthrie looked meaningfully at Pritchard, and they were both grinning.

'Well, well. Where was that?' Pritchard asked Corey nicely.

Corey sighed. 'Over at Texas State Prison. We just got out.'

Guthrie shook his head. 'By Jesus. Gabriel might double our salary after this one, partner. We got a sure thing this time.'

Sumner saw it was getting out of hand fast. 'Look. Take us to the Spencer house. The boy will tell you it wasn't Corey. Then this can be over.'

Guthrie shook his ugly head. 'What if the Spencer boy says he can't identify him? He might be scared to do it. And then we'd lose that nice little raise we been hoping for. Right, Duke?'

Pritchard grinned. 'That would be like throwing money down a black hole,' he said in a guttural tone. 'OK, partner. Let's cuff them.'

Guthrie took handcuffs out and cuffed Sumner, still holding the Colt on him with his other hand. Pritchard took a bit longer to get his cuffs, and then he grabbed Corey and turned him around. 'Right, boy killer. You're going to answer now for what you done.'

But Corey was wild with panic. Before Pritchard could secure the handcuffs, he swung back around and threw a fist at Pritchard's square face.

The blow connected but not solidly. 'Corey!' Sumner yelled at him.

But it was too late. Pritchard's face was a mask of rage. In a quick moment he slammed his Colt into Corey's head, hitting him on the left temple. Corey gasped and slumped to the ground, dazed. Pritchard had a frenzied look in his eyes, and blood ran from his mouth. As Sumner and Guthrie watched, Pritchard went over to Corey and kicked him savagely in the side.

'Hey!' Sumner called out angrily.

Guthrie was grinning.

Now Pritchard was picking up a four-foot length of a dead branch that had fallen to the ground. It was thick with no real offshoots except a few stubs remaining. He hefted it out once and then slammed it down onto Corey's back. The club cracked against Corey's ribs, and the sharp stubs dug into his flesh through his shirt. Corey screamed out in harsh pain that seemed to rocket through his whole body.

'You little weasel,' Pritchard was muttering. Breathlessly. Then he swung the wicked club again onto Corey's back and head. A lesser cry came from Corey.

Sumner was on his way over there halfway through Pritchard's second swing of the club. 'You goddamn animal!' In a low growl. Pritchard was caught off-guard by the launched attack and Sumner hit him bodily, hands cuffed behind him.

They went down together, but Sumner's hands were useless. He had wanted to make Pritchard stop. As soon as he hit the ground with Pritchard, though, he felt the barrel of Guthrie's Colt slam against the back of his head, and bright lights flashed on inside his skull and he fell off Pritchard. He was semi-conscious, with a deep moan coming from his throat.

Pritchard got awkwardly to his feet, crimson-faced. He drew his own Colt and aimed it at Sumner's head.

'No, wait,' Guthrie said quickly.

'What the hell for?' Pritchard grated out.

'We shoot them now, it's over,' Guthrie reasoned smoothly with his cohort. 'You don't want that.'

Pritchard re-aimed the revolver. 'Also,' Guthrie added carefully, 'this will all make a bigger impression on Judge Gabriel if we bring them to trial. We'll get a lot more attention. And credit.' He said the last slowly.

Sumner could hear them talking but couldn't make much sense of it. Pritchard stood there breathing hard for a moment then viciously jammed the Colt back into its holster. Then he picked up the club again and rained two more savage blows onto barely-conscious Corey, fracturing two posterior ribs and a low vertebra in Corey's back. There had been one more muffled outcry from Corey, then he was unconscious.

Pritchard threw the club down, and kicked Corey's left thigh. His face still twisted up with emotion.

'That's enough,' Guthrie said casually. He had enjoyed watching it. 'You'll kill 'em, and spoil it for us down in Fort Sill.'

Pritchard hesitated, then nodded. 'I got most of it out of me. There won't never be two pieces of pond scum I'll enjoy watching hang than these two.'

Sumner was coming around. He glanced at Corey's still form and felt a heavy weight in his chest. He sat up groggily, his hands still cuffed.

'Oh. You ain't dead, neither.' Guthrie grinned. 'Good.'

'You bastards,' Sumner snapped. 'If he isn't dead, he might be soon. He's an innocent boy.'

They both ignored him. 'I'll throw this one across his saddle,' Pritchard said to Guthrie. 'And get his butt on board.'

He walked over to Sumner who had just struggled to his feet. He looked directly into Sumner's eyes, then threw a big fist into his face. There was the sound of bone breaking in Sumner's nose, and then he was on the ground again. He lay there gasping, hatred in his blue eyes, blood inching from his nose.

'Now all out of me,' Pritchard growled. 'Get him saddled up and we'll get riding. We got a long trail ahead of us.'

It was an overnight ride to Fort Sill. The rest of that day seemed like a week to Sumner, as he rode along behind the two lawmen, hands cuffed in front of him now and tied to the saddle horn of his mount. Beside him on the other roan was Corey, his body hanging over the mount's flanks on either side. Occasionally a low moan would come from Corey's throat, so Sumner knew he was alive. But Sumner worried that the long ride would make his injuries worse, or even kill him.

When they camped that night, Corey was taken off the horse and slung to the ground without a groundsheet under him, and Sumner was seated against a young mesquite sapling all night with first Guthrie watching over him, and then Pritchard.

There was no possibility of escape for Sumner. Anyway, he would not have left his new friend. He had visions of pleading their case before a judge, and having someone finally listen to them.

The next morning, Corey opened his eyes and moved, then cried out in pain. Guthrie gave him a cup of water and most of it fell onto Corey's bloodied shirt. Sumner was watching from a few feet away. Guthrie helped Corey to sit up and Corey spotted Sumner.

'Sumner!' He choked a little. 'What happened?'

'Don't talk, kid. It will be all right.'

'The hell it will.' Pritchard grinned from a small distance. He was saddling up, not far from Sumner.

'You boys will pay for this,' Sumner muttered quietly.

'No. We'll get paid for it.' Guthrie chuckled.

Soon they were on their way again, and now Corey was set onto his saddle, and that relieved Sumner's tension some. But it was obvious Corey was in constant pain, and by mid-morning he was just slumped over his saddle horn, barely able to stay aboard the horse. Through a long day of agony for Corey, the foursome arrived in Fort Sill around mid-afternoon.

It was a fairly good sized town, with a wide central square, like a Mexican plaza with government buildings and shops all around its perimeter. The first thing that caught Sumner's eye was the hanging scaffold that stood right in front of the court house and jail. The heaviness came back into his chest. He looked over at Corey, but Corey's head was hanging and he was taking notice of nothing.

'Take a good look, Sumner.' Guthrie grinned at him. 'It's just setting there waiting for you two.'

At the building, a cup of water was thrown onto Corey's face, and it brought him around. 'What's going on, Sumner?' he mumbled.

'We're here,' Sumner told him. 'We'll get to see a judge now and we'll be all right.'

Pritchard and Guthrie exchanged a knowing look. And then they got Corey and Sumner off their mounts. Corey could barely stand.

'All right, you two slabs of horse pucky,' Pritchard

barked at them. 'You got a date with the judge later. But for now we got a real nice little cell all ready for you. I reckon you know all about cells, huh?'

Within a few minutes, they were locked into a cell very much like the one they had shared in Texas except this one smelled of ammonia and there were no rat droppings on the floor. They asked for water and got it, and an hour later they were served trays of edible food. Sumner wolfed his down, his head still aching from the pistol whipping administered by Guthrie. The meal was beans and bread, and Sumner forced Corey to eat some of it. Corey tried for a few minutes, and then quit.

'My back,' he said to Sumner. 'I need something for the pain, Sumner. And I think there's something broke inside me. I feel kind of sick.'

Sumner swallowed hard. 'I'll get you some help, Corey.'

In late afternoon they did tape Corey's ribs, and someone brought him some laudanum. About a half hour later, a guard came and took them up a flight of stairs and down a corridor to the court room.

Judge Gabriel was seated on the bench. There was no black robe. He looked more like a rancher sitting in for a judge. He slumped on a high-backed chair, and a flask of whiskey stood before him on the bench. Pritchard and Guthrie sat in front row seats, and there was a court reporter and bailiff present.

The federal judges in the Territory, when one existed there, were notorious for their abbreviated trials, and lack of formal procedure, and Gabriel was the most egregious of them since the other infamous Hanging Judge Parker. Justice was swift in the Territory, and its sometimes questionable deputies operated more like the *federales* across the Mexican border than lawmen on the US side.

Corey and Sumner were seated at a table for defendants before the bench, and the bailiff announced their separate charges. An elderly court reporter sat before the bench and took everything down in shorthand.

'Just relax, Corey,' Sumner spoke quietly to him. Corey looked as if he might fall off his chair at any moment.

Judge Gabriel took a short swig from the whiskey bottle and then stowed it in a drawer out of view. He leaned forward onto the mahogany bench before him and clasped his hands on it.

'Well. What have we here?' Squinting toward the two defendants. 'Are these the killers you told me about, Deputies?'

'Yes, sir,' Guthrie answered for them.

Gabriel put a hand up and covered a belch. 'All right. We've got one Corey Madison here, and a Wesley Sumner. Which one of you is Madison?'

Corey wasn't paying any attention. 'That's Corey beside me here, Your Honor,' Sumner spoke up for him. 'He's not feeling very well right now.'

Gabriel scowled at Sumner. 'I guess you're his partner in crime.'

'We committed no crime, Your Honor.'

'Then you're both pleading not guilty?'

Sumner shot a quick glance at Corey. Corey looked at him drunkenly. 'Yes, sir,' Sumner answered for them.

Gabriel sighed, and focused on Corey. 'Boy, you'd scare crows out of a turnip patch. What the hell happened to you? You look like you been run over by a gut wagon.'

'Maybe you should ask them,' Sumner said acidly,

gesturing toward Pritchard and Guthrie. 'Sir.'

Pritchard stood up. 'That boy resisted arrest, Your Honor. It took us a few minutes to subdue him.'

'You damn near beat him to death!' Sumner said loudly.

Gabriel took a gavel and pounded with it a couple of times. 'All right. Let's keep some order in here.' There were a half dozen spectators scattered through the room, and Sumner heard one of them laugh softly.

'You ought to learn to cooperate with the law, Madison,' Gabriel finally continued.

'Well, you boys will be heard separately, but that should pose no problem time-wise. You'll be first, Madison. Are you represented by counsel?'

Corey focused on him. 'Huh?' he murmured. He moved an arm and emitted a low cry of pain.

'We don't know any lawyers here,' Sumner said.

Gabriel chuckled. 'It would surprise me if you did. We buried the last one a week ago. He took the influenza.'

This time the chuckle came from Guthrie.

'The thing is,' Gabriel went on, 'I've heard the evidence against you, Mr Madison, and it's pretty conclusive. We got the testimony of these two officers behind you on record already. Now we're ready to hear your side, Madison. Sumner, I'll listen to you tomorrow. I've got an appointment at the local saloon in a half hour. A matter of business, of course.' He grinned and the two deputy marshals returned it.

'We haven't had a chance to hear what they said,' Sumner objected.

Gabriel gave him a hard look. 'What are you, Mr Sumner? One of them Philadelphia lawyers? We don't worry about cross-examination and all that New York procedure here in the Territory. We just listen to both sides and make a decision. And get on to the next case. You understand me?'

Sumner tried to suppress the new anger rising in him. 'Yes. I'm beginning to.'

'Do you want to make a statement under oath, Mr Madison?' Gabriel continued.

Corey stared up at him. 'I don't feel good. I want to go home.'

Gabriel shook his head. 'I don't have time for this.'

'May I speak for him?' Sumner asked him.

Gabriel sighed. 'Fine. But make it fast.'

Sumner took a deep breath in. 'Like we told these two behind us, we were nowhere near the Spencer farm the night that murder happened. We were camping on the trail, on our way to the Prescott ranch to talk about work. We offered to ride there and prove it. And we didn't have the money on us that was stolen.'

Gabriel had been cleaning a fingernail through that summary. He now looked down on Sumner narrowly. 'Is that it?'

Sumner hesitated. 'Yes, Your Honor.'

'And that's pretty much your defence, too?'

Sumner nodded. Gabriel looked down at a paper. 'All right.' He turned his attention to Corey. 'Will the defendant Corey Madison please rise?'

Corey didn't even hear him. Sumner pulled Corey to his feet as gently as he could, making Corey wince. Corey almost slumped out of Sumner's grasp.

'Corey Madison, this court finds you guilty as charged and sentences you to hang by the neck until you are dead.'

'What!' Sumner yelled out.

'Your execution will take place tomorrow morning at dawn, here in the public square.' He pounded the gavel and rose. 'Take the prisoner away.'

Sumner couldn't believe it. 'No, wait! We want an appeal!'

'We don't allow appeals from this court.' Gabriel frowned at him. 'I'll see you tomorrow, Mr Sumner.'

'This is a goddamn outrage!' Sumner yelled.

But Gabriel was gone. The bailiff, a large, square man, ushered them from the court room and a guard from the jail took charge of them outside and returned them to their cell. Corey almost fell down twice on the way, with Sumner keeping him on his feet.

Once back in the cell and with Corey collapsed on his lower cot, Sumner sat heavily onto the edge of it and put his head in his hands. His mouth tasted like old paper, and his head throbbed. He looked over at Corey, who looked asleep but with a rattle in his throat. Sumner was still trying to understand how things could have gone so terribly wrong in such a brief time. He couldn't get it through his head that they were actually going to hang this innocent boy tomorrow, whose sister back in Texas was blithely awaiting his return from his work foray with good news for them.

When blackness showed in the high barred window of their cell, Sumner climbed onto the upper bunk and tried to fall asleep. Thinking of what was going to happen at dawn. Feeling as if he were in the middle of a nightmare that he might wake up from at any moment and be back in hardship camp with Corey, looking forward to their separate futures.

He couldn't sleep. He climbed back down and began pacing the floor of the tiny cell.

Wondering if there was something he could do to derail what was about to happen.

At an hour when dawn seemed not far distant, Sumner leant against the wall opposite the bunks, when there was suddenly a loud croaking noise coming from Corey's throat. Sumner rushed over there and grabbed Corey.

'Corey! Look at me! Are you all right?'

As he held his friend, a loud coughing started, and in a moment it was worse, and then wet crimson erupted from Corey's mouth, some spraying onto Sumner's shirt. Then a great rattling came, and after that Corey stopped breathing. Sumner couldn't believe it.

'Corey! Goddamn it, kid! Breathe!'

But Corey's body was lifeless. And slowly growing cool to the touch. Sumner sat there, breathing hard now. A burning hatred starting in him, many times greater than it had been in court. And something settled hard inside him that he sensed would never go away. A new hardness, greater than anything at the Texas prison, toward the potential ugliness of his world. Toward those men of the law in that court room. And men like them everywhere.

He was still sitting over Corey when they came at dawn and uttered their exclamations of surprise when they saw Corey.

'Well, if that don't beat all,' the second one in said.

'He died about an hour ago,' Sumner said heavily.

The other man grunted. 'I guess he really didn't want to go out there this morning.' A narrow grin.

44

Sumner ignored it, rising to his feet. 'When will you take him?'

The guard who had just spoken shrugged. 'That's up to Gabriel. But for now, we'll have to move you over to the next cell. It's the rules.'

It was almost two hours later – while Corey's body grew stiff in the adjacent cell – when a single guard came to take Sumner to his court appearance. He tried to get a last look at Corey, but failed.

Sumner was still so distracted by events that he was barely aware of arriving in the court room. His face was grim, his posture slumped. He had prepared himself mentally for the sentence of hanging.

Gabriel sat behind the bench, talking and laughing softly with a different bailiff. The same aged court reporter sat ready to record proceedings. When Gabriel saw Sumner being led in, he dismissed the bailiff, and that slim fellow descended to floor level. Gabriel eyed Sumner silently as Sumner was seated at an inset table. The bailiff announced the court to be in session. Today there were about three dozen spectators, most from the disappointed crowd outside in the square.

'Well, Mr Sumner,' Gabriel began. He looked unkempt, as if he were suffering from the effects of excessive drinking. 'I hear that your partner Mr Madison has managed to escape the gallows.'

Sumner heard feet scraping behind him, and turned slightly to see Pritchard and Guthrie seat themselves in the front row of seats again.

'These men killed him,' Sumner said bitterly. 'Just as sure as if they'd put a bullet in him, I guess this way was better entertainment for them.'

'That's a goddamn lie!' Pritchard said loudly in his deep voice.

Gabriel blew his cheeks out. It was obvious he didn't want to be there.

'Gentlemen. I'd like to proceed,' he said irritably.

'Yes, let's get it over with,' Sumner grumbled. 'While your hangman is still available out there.'

Gabriel sighed heavily. 'You don't make it easy for me, boy.'

'I didn't know I was supposed to,' Sumner retorted.

Gabriel ignored the response. 'I've been reviewing these deputies' statements,' he went on. 'The Spencer boy saw just one man running from his house to a mount not far away. When asked, he thought there was no other person with him.'

Sumner just stood there, wondering where this was going.

'These boys just brought you in to get this all settled here in court,' Gabriel went on. 'Even though Madison fit the description of the thief and was obviously guilty, I can't find enough hard evidence against you individually to hang you.'

'Hell,' Guthrie muttered, from behind Sumner.

'In fact, because I'm in a good mood today,' Gabriel smiled wanly, 'I'm not going to try to keep you here for conspiracy. I'm already bored with this case. I'm releasing you from custody and you're free to ride back to Texas and cause some other judge trouble there.'

Sumner frowned slightly. He couldn't believe he had heard properly. 'The charge against me is dropped?' he said quietly.

'That's correct,' Gabriel said blithely. 'Bailiff, remove

his handcuffs and escort him from the building. If I ever see you here again, Sumner, I'll hang you on general principles. This court is adjourned until 1:30 this afternoon.'

'You lucky sonofabitch,' Pritchard grated out, just at his left shoulder.

As the judge retired to his chambers, the bailiff came and took Sumner's cuffs off, and Sumner rubbed his wrists. He still couldn't believe what was happening. It was almost as bizarre as Corey's death.

'I'd like to claim Corey's body,' Sumner told the bailiff. 'To take it back to his sister in Texas.'

'Oh, that won't be possible,' the other man said. 'He's already being buried up at Boot Hill this morning. Under court order.'

Sumner slumped inside himself.

'Too bad, trail bum.' From behind him.

He turned around and saw Guthrie's grinning face. Pritchard's still showed mild anger, at Sumner's release.

'Maybe they'll give you his spurs,' Pritchard said acidly.

'Or his boots, if you can take the stink,' Guthrie offered. They both laughed.

Sumner stood there silent for a moment. 'I think you boys are under a wrong impression here. Do you really think you're going to get away with this?'

His voice was calm, self-assured. Deadly serious. Pritchard looked into those cold blue eyes and saw something there he didn't like, and the feeling he got from that look angered him. 'Why, you no-good Texas trash, I think you need another lesson in manners.' In a hard, grating voice. He started for Sumner.

47

But Guthrie's hand grabbed him. 'No. Gabriel wouldn't like it. Just let him go. I'm sick of his face.'

Sumner gave a half smile. A smile with resolve and rock-steady grit behind it. 'A day will come I'll be back in the Territory. When I'm ready. When the time is right. And I'll be looking for you. Both of you.'

'I ever see you again, you goddamn worm, I'll shoot you on sight!' Pritchard yelled at him.

'And then we'll leave your carcass for the buzzards to feed on,' Guthrie said breathlessly.

Sumner elbowed past them and left the building. By noon, he had retrieved his horse and was riding out. Heading back to Texas.

CHAPTER THREE

Sumner rode hard that first day out of Fort Sill, wanting to put it as far behind him as possible. He rode through arid, desolate country for a few hours, sweating heavily. By late afternoon he had crossed over into Texas.

It was less than another hour when he came to a little village called Butte Junction. It was mostly just a hot wide single street lined with stores, two storey houses, a tiny hotel and a saloon. Sumner was exhausted. He stopped at the saloon, tied the roan to a long hitching post, and went inside.

When he got in there, he saw the place was already fairly crowded prior to the evening's rush. He ordered a beer, and ate a complimentary boiled egg with it. As he was finishing the egg, a cowpoke from a nearby table called out to him. 'Hey, mister! We need a fourth over here for poker. Want to get rich?'

Sumner hesitated. He had just a few dollars. But if he won, he might be able to afford a room at the hotel down the street. He shrugged, and walked with his beer over to the table. 'Boys, I can sit in a couple of hands, I reckon.'

'Take some weight off.' The cowpoke grinned. 'These

two boys are already bankrupting me. This one over here from our ranch.' He indicated a lanky cowboy. 'That one works for the place here.' He gestured toward the fourth man at a table, a professional gambler employed by the saloon. The cowboy nodded, but the gambler just gave Sumner a narrow, sober look.

'My pleasure,' Sumner said quietly, as he seated himself. 'But don't take me down too fast, boys. I have a horse to feed.'

The cowboy who had invited him over laughed, and then started a deal. Around the room there was a lot of loud talking and laughing, and a small man at the far rear was pounding out a tinny tune on an old piano. At the bar, voices were raised for a moment, and then a drunken cowboy threw a punch at another man and the fellow went down and stayed there. Both cowpokes at Sumner's table laughed loudly, but the gambler just shook his head.

'All right boys,' the dealer was saying. 'That's the best I can do for you. Make your bets and hold your breath.'

The gambler won the first hand. The other players grumbled a bit, and then the other cowboy was dealing. Sumner got three aces and won the hand. A satisfied look crossed his face. He could get a hotel room now, if he didn't lose it back to them. When the gambler dealt, he won again but then Sumner won the next three hands. He was getting great cards. At his last win, he had a small pile of coins and paper money before him.

'You been giving me some good cards,' he told the table. 'I might just call it a night. I want to see if there's a room left at the hotel down the street.'

But suddenly there was a revolver in the gambler's

hand, and he was scowling at Sumner. 'You ain't going nowhere, trail drifter.'

The two cowboys looked solemnly at him, and at a couple of tables close by, the drinkers stopped talking and turned to see the gun in the gambler's hand.

'Hey, Murdoch.' The first cowboy frowned. 'What's the matter?'

'How have you been getting all them good hands?' Murdoch asked Sumner in a low voice. 'You working a system on us, boy?'

Sumner sighed and shook his head. 'I don't know any systems. You boys been giving me those cards. What I won was fair and square. And you can put that gun away, mister. As you can see, I'm not carrying.'

'I can get you a gun,' Murdoch growled. 'Why ain't you armed? Afraid somebody will shoot you for stealing their money?'

The entire room had quieted down now, and the piano had gone silent.

'I just got out of prison,' Sumner replied evenly, holding the other man's brittle gaze. 'I haven't had a chance to get one yet.'

All three looked at him differently. 'Was you at that State Prison down south of here?' the cowboy said who invited Sumner.

Sumner nodded, and swigged the last of his beer. 'That's right.'

'Wait a minute,' Murdoch said. 'You ain't that boy that took down Walcott and them other two murderers? About seven, eight years ago?'

Sumner sighed. 'You got me nailed, I guess.'

'Sumner,' Murdoch said to himself. 'Wesley, ain't it?'

'I'm sorry my reputation precedes me.'

Murdoch holstered his revolver, 'Well, I'll be damned.'

'I shot them down in cold blood,' Sumner said softly.

'Jesus!' the second cowpoke said in a half-whisper.

'Them low-lifes got just what they deserved,' Murdoch said. 'That sonofabitch Walcott murdered my older brother for some petty cash in his cabin. I was looking for him, too.'

'He raped and murdered my aunt,' Sumner said. And it occurred to him in that moment that Judge Gabriel had never asked him why he had been in Texas State Prison. If he had, Sumner figured, Sumner might have swung from the scaffold outside the jail.

'If that bastard didn't go to hell, there ain't no use having one,' Murdoch muttered.

'Glad you feel that way,' Sumner told him. 'Some folks took it bad, the way it happened.'

'Some folks got clabber for brains,' Murdoch spat out.

The two cowboys were surprised at the quick turn of events. The noise in the saloon had increased again and the piano player was banging out 'Dixie' to the delight of most patrons.

'Well,' the second cowboy said brightly. 'Why don't I deal out another hand?'

Murdoch gathered in the cash in front of him and looked over at Sumner. 'I got a better idea. Why don't you grab your winnings, Sumner, and let me buy you one up at the bar?'

Sumner shrugged, and raked in his money. 'Sure. That hotel room will wait a little.'

'Find us some more players!' the first cowpoke called

after them as they left.

Up at the long bar, Murdoch found a place where they would be more private and Sumner joined him there. Murdoch ordered them two Planter's Rye whiskeys without asking Sumner. In a moment the glasses were delivered, and Murdoch raised his glass to Sumner. He was a brawny man with pock marks on his lower face.

'Here's to the death of a snake!'

Sumner drank with him and they both leaned against the bar. 'Sorry I kind of lost my temper back there. I been cheated by a couple of drifters lately. No offense.'

'None taken,' Sumner said. 'You play a sweet game of poker.'

Murdoch grinned. 'I been at it a while.' He looked Sumner over. 'You're pretty young to have all that behind you.'

Sumner sighed. 'It all caught me young.'

'Now that you're out, you got plans for your future?'

Sumner didn't respond for a moment. 'Not really. There's a stage line where I'm headed. I might see if they want a driver. Or ride out to one of the nearby ranches.'

Murdoch looked over at him. 'You'd make a good ranch hand. If you're heading south, you'll ride right past a ranch of an old friend of mine. Name of Clay Allison.'

Sumner frowned at him. 'Clay Allison? You mean the gunfighter?'

Murdoch grinned. 'He learned to shoot in the Confederate Army. Sure, there's stories about him. Hot-tempered shootings in saloon fights. They say him and a farmer neighbour argued over a fence line. On Clay's suggestion, they dug a grave right there and both got into it, and shot it out in that hole in the ground. Only Clay climbed back out of that hole.'

Sumner shook his head, smiling.

'Some of them yarns might be bull-pucky. But one thing is true. Clay Allison is the fastest damn gun in this whole state.'

'I'm impressed,' Sumner said, taking a drink of the Planter's.

'Of course, now that he's got his ranch, he's settled right down. Although he does raise a little hell now and again.' He grinned pensively. 'Anyway, I just heard he's looking for a couple of new hires for handyman work. I think you might fill the bill and you can say I recommended you.'

Sumner caught his gaze and fixed on it. When that gun was aimed at his chest at the table, he would never have guessed that this rough-looking gambler would be offering to help him with his future.

'I'm mighty obliged,' Sumner told him. 'I might just take you up on that.'

'You tell him Murdoch sent you,' the gambler said, swigging the rye. 'I think you'll like old Clay.'

Sumner's thoughts flashed momentarily to the Madison farm, and Corey, and the grim task that lay ahead of him before he could consider his future. 'We'll see how it works out,' he said noncommittally.

The night at the hotel was very necessary to restore Sumner. By dawn the next day, he was on his way south to Blaneyville and the Madison farm. The land was a little more hospitable here in Texas with more cottonwoods and plane trees dotting the landscape. There were also more ranches and he rode through small herds of cattle several times on his way south. As he came nearer to the Madison farm, the weight in his chest grew heavier with each mile he covered.

Around mid-morning, the farm house came into view.

Sumner reined in and studied it for a moment. It looked so peaceful. So idyllic in its tranquillity. And now he was going to destroy all that in a moment. He dreaded this as much as he had dreaded the gallows at Fort Sill.

Sumner rode on up to the house, and saw a horse tethered to a short hitching cost outside. He dismounted heavily and left the roan at the post. He climbed three steps up to the small porch and called inside past an open doorway.

'Hallo, inside!'

In a moment Jane Madison appeared at the door, her lovely face looking puzzled. Then she broke into a big smile that cut Sumner`s insides.

'Wesley Sumner!' She reached up and hugged him. 'I thought it was about time for you two to be back!' She looked past him. 'Where's Corey?' Eager expectation on her face.

'He's not with me, Jane,' he said quietly.

'What? Where is he then?' she asked, not understanding.

'Maybe we'd better go inside,' he suggested.

Now she frowned, and gave another look behind him. 'Oh. All right.'

They went in together, and there was an elderly man standing in the parlour, eyeing Sumner curiously.

'This is Wesley Sumner, Gramps,' Jane announced him. 'Wesley, this is my grandfather. He's been staying with me until Corey's return.'

The weight in Sumner's chest lightened almost imperceptibly. 'Glad to meet you, sir,' Sumner told him.

Her grandfather, Bias Driscoll, stuck his hand out and Sumner took it. 'Glad to meet you, boy. I hear you're Corey's friend.'

Sumner took a deep breath in. 'Maybe we all better sit down for a moment.'

Now a small concern appeared on Jane's pretty face. They all sat at a sofa and big chair, Sumner facing them. He clasped his hands before him.

'What is it, Wesley?' Jane asked him wanly. She was the only one since his aunt to use his first name.

Sumner realized there was no easy way for them. 'Corey won't be returning home, Jane. Your brother is dead.'

Jane's pretty face drained of color.

'Good God!' Driscoll breathed.

Sumner told them the whole story. Slowly, painfully, Jane listened to the entire narrative in silence. Then the three of them just sat there.

Jane finally rose from the sofa, turned and took three steps across the parlour, and collapsed to the floor.

Sumner and Driscoll were over her in a moment, Driscoll patting her cheek lightly. 'Jane! Janie! Oh, Jesus!'

'She'll be all right, Mr Driscoll,' Sumner assured him. 'It's just temporary shock. Let's get her to bed.'

Sumner carried Jane into a bedroom on the main floor of the big house, and she came around a little. Driscoll brought her a glass of water, which she refused. 'Just let me rest,' she whispered.

Jane remained in bed for the next twenty-four hours, taking just a few swallows of broth in the meantime. Sumner helped Driscoll with chores, chopping kindling wood, repairing a window shutter. Washing dishes. On the second day, Jane was back up, making them a late breakfast and then sitting with them quietly at the kitchen table.

'You look better,' Sumner offered as they sat drinking black coffee.

'I feel like I was run over by a conestoga,' Jane admitted. She stared past them. 'I can't get it straight in my head. That I'll never see him again. Why didn't I take a longer look at him when he rode off?'

'They was real close,' Driscoll confided to Sumner. 'When they was little, they did everything together. They was joined at the hip.'

'I never had that closeness with anybody,' Sumner said.

'It makes it harder when it's taken from you,' Jane murmured, her eyes tearing up.

'Time will help,' Sumner said.

'I can't run this farm alone,' Jane said, sipping at her coffee. The aroma of it filled the room, and was a small warm counterpoint to the heaviness that hung over them.

'I already decided,' Driscoll told her. 'I'm going to move my things in here for a while. Maybe permanent. I ain't working my little patch of ground anyhow. I might as well be over here where I can do some good.'

'You quit on your place because you didn't want to do it any more,' Jane reminded him.

'I feel different about it now. This gives me a purpose.

A man needs a purpose, you know. Anyway, that Seger boy that hangs around you all the time. I bet he'd be happy as a pig in mud to help out here.'

'Seger?' Sumner said.

'A neighbour not far off,' Jane said. She gave a slow look at Sumner. 'One of Corey's friends.'

'He's sweet on Janie,' Driscoll put in.

'While you and Corey was gone,' Jane said, holding Sumner's gaze, 'the crazy boy asked me to marry him.' After assessing Sumner's reaction, she turned away quickly.

Sumner was surprised. He had to admit that he had thought a lot of lovely Jane while he was away. 'What did you tell him?'

'Oh, that's the third time he tried. I just keep saying I'm not ready.'

'For marriage?'

'For marriage to him.' She looked back at him with those big blue eyes, and he saw something there through the pain for Corey.

He looked quickly away. 'I see.'

Driscoll looked from her to him, and smiled. 'I think I'll just go throw down some chicken feed,' he said.

No more was said between them, though. In the next few days, Sumner stayed on to make sure Jane was all right. Driscoll gave him some work clothes that fit pretty well, and by the third day Sumner was ready to ride. The young man Hank Seger stopped by that morning and he was a big, strapping man who seemed a good-natured fellow who could make a woman a decent husband. He kept giving Sumner suspicious looks throughout his brief visit. When Sumner and Jane were alone at the kitchen table again, he caught her gaze and smiled.

'You could do worse,' he said.

'Hank?'

'I kind of liked him.'

Jane narrowed her eyes on him. 'So you think I should marry him?' A little hostilely.

Sumner frowned. 'I didn't say that. Look, Jane.'

'I thought you knew when you left here. That there was something between us. That you felt it, too. Was I wrong?'

Sumner sighed. She was right. He really liked this girl. From the first time she had smiled at him. 'I started to tell you. I have plans that stretch out quite a spell. And it involves those men that killed Corey.'

'What do you mean?'

He met her troubled look. 'I better not say much more. I'm heading out today for the Allison ranch.'

'For permanent work?'

'Let's just say it's a first step in a plan.'

Her eyes were moist again. 'Today? You don't have to do anything, you know. If I can handle this, you ought to be able to.'

'You weren't there,' he said evenly.

She turned away from him. 'Then you don't care about me.'

'That isn't true. I'll be back. I promise that.'

She rose angrily. 'All right! Go, damn it! If I've lost both of you, I'll have to live with it!'

Sumner stood up. 'Jane. I do have feelings for you. And I will come back.'

'I'll just fetch your riding jacket,' she said coolly.

*

The Clay Allison ranch was an overnight ride, not far from Las Animas. When Sumner arrived in the afternoon of the following day, he was dusty, hungry and tired. He rode through a large herd of cattle on his way in, all with the Allison brand, and finally he found himself in front of a rambling ranch house. He hitched his roan there and noted that the animal was lame. When he climbed the steps of a wide porch, a lanky man was just emerging from inside. He looked Sumner over carefully.

'Where did you come from, boy?' In an arrogant tone.

Sumner ignored his manner, wiping a hand across his forehead. 'I'm here to see Mr Allison. A fellow named Murdoch sent me.'

The other man frowned. He was Tom Bedford and he was Allison's ranch foreman. He had a lean hard look, and wore a sidearm low on his hip. 'You know Murdoch?'

Sumner nodded. 'He said he thought Mr Allison might be hiring.'

Bedford looked him over with disdain. 'You don't look like no cowpoke.'

Sumner sighed. 'I'm not. Yet. Is he here today?'

Bedford grunted. 'Sure. He's here. Come on inside.'

They entered and walked down a carpeted hallway to a closed door, and Bedford knocked lightly on it. A deep voice called out to enter. Bedford led Sumner into the big room, which was dominated by a wide fireplace on the opposite wall, with a fire crackling there. A large, well-dressed man with silver in his sideburns and wide brawny shoulders sat at a small desk to their left. He looked up impatiently.

'What is it, Bedford?' He sat back and looked Sumner over.

'This here boy says Murdoch sent him to look for work here.' A sly grin.

Allison's face showed curiosity. He rose from the desk and came around it. 'Murdoch, huh? How's that old chicken thief looking these days?'

'He looked like he can handle himself,' Sumner told him.

Allison grinned, and nodded. 'That will be all, Bedford. Go see to that lame heifer out back. I want it back out in pasture.'

'He ain't got no experience,' Bedford said, jerking his head toward Sumner.

Allison frowned slightly. 'The heifer, Bedford.'

Bedford looked a bit frustrated. 'Yes, sir.' He gave Sumner a sour look, and turned and left.

Allison came over to Sumner and looked him over openly. He looked very physical for his age. He wore two bone-handled Colts low on his hips, a red shirt, and a flowing blue cravat at his neck. He was known all over Texas and Arizona for his gunplay, and Sumner wondered how many men those guns had sent to hell.

'How do you know Murdoch, son?' he asked Sumner.

'Only through a card game,' Sumner said.

'Don't you ever carry a gun?'

'I haven't had a chance to arm myself,' Sumner said. 'Since I got out.'

'Out of what?' Allison inquired.

Sumner hesitated. 'Out of State Prison.'

Allison's face went sober and he looked Sumner over more carefully.

'I shot three men down that murdered my aunt. The name is Sumner. Wesley Sumner.'

Allison nodded. 'I remember. Three goddamn piles of cow flop. You rid the world of a wagonload of trash there. I wish I'd done it myself. I hope they're all in hell with their backs broke.' He stuck his thick hand out. 'Pleasured to meet up with you, Sumner.'

Sumner shook his hand, and felt the iron in it. 'I'm honored, sir.'

'Call me Clay,' Allison told him. 'I think we might be kindred spirits.'

Sumner grinned. 'All right.'

'As a matter of fact, I have been thinking of taking on a new hand or two. I don't care that you got no experience. I can teach you all I know in about five minutes.' A broad grin. 'And don't pay no attention to Bedford. That head is empty as last year's crow's nest.'

Sumner smiled. 'We'll get along. And I appreciate the hire, Mr – I mean, Clay.' He paused. 'But I like you, so I have to level with you. This would be temporary employment for me. I'll enjoy ranch work, I think. But there was something else I was hoping to learn.'

Allison frowned at him. 'Something else?'

Sumner held his look with a steady one. 'I want you to teach me about guns, Clay.'

Allison just stood there for a long moment, then he squinted. 'Why hell, boy. You took down three of the worst misfits this state has ever seen.'

'I was a crazy kid with a debt to collect,' Sumner said. 'I shot them down in cold blood. I murdered them.'

Allison nodded thoughtfully.

'And the law made me pay for it,' Sumner added. 'I want to be able to face a fast gun down and kill him. Legally.'

Allison eyed him sidewise. 'Have anybody particular in mind?'

Sumner looked away. 'Two men. Over in the Territory. They killed a friend of mine. They're US Deputy Marshals.'

Allison's beefy face showed surprise for a moment. Then a wide smile came across it. 'I knew I was going to like you.'

'I figure that even after you've shown me all you can, it will take me a while until I know what I'm doing. But sooner or later, I'm going back.'

Allison clapped him on the shoulder. 'Well, that might be a long time from now. In the meantime, let's give you some ranching know-how. I won't put you out on the range yet. I'll start you on repairing fences. Extending the corral. Maybe some personal work for me.'

'I'm ready to start today,' Sumner told him.

'Sunbreak tomorrow will be fine. Today I'll get you bedded down out in the bunkhouse. And introduce you to the boys.'

Sumner was accepted readily by the other ranch-hands and cowboys, despite his background. The foreman Bedford barely spoke to him, but fortunately they had little contact. Sumner began doing odd jobs about the ranch, and only rarely any range work like rounding up strays. Bedford would occasionally give him some unwarranted criticism, and Sumner made no objection.

When he had been there just under a week, the roan's lameness got worse, and Allison put the animal out to pasture and presented Sumner with a beautiful black stallion with white markings on its forehead and two feet.

Sumner loved it at first sight, and bought a dark saddle for it that was already fitted with a rifle scabbard.

In the third week, Allison bought Sumner a brand new Colt .45 Peacemaker complete with a holster and gun-belt. All of this came out of Sumner's pay but he had nothing else to spend his money on anyway. At the end of that week, Allison began taking Sumner out behind a big barn and showing him all about the Colt, and how to use it. He wasn't an easy teacher.

'No, no! Squeeze the damn trigger! You're still pulling at it! Eyes wide open! Keep that shooting arm straight as a ramrod! Don't see anything but the bullseye!' The targets were fifty yards away.

At the end of the summer, Sumner could hit a half dollar that Allison threw into the air before it hit the ground. And hit a bullseye at fifty yards nine out of ten times.

In the fall: 'You're wearing that beautiful gun too damn high! Too much elbow action. You trying to do acrobatics, or draw a gun?'

And so it went. Fall came and a light winter. One spring day, Allison came to him and said, 'Let's see your draw.'

'Maybe it's too soon to show anything.'

'Come on, I seen you practising. Show me what you got.'

They faced each other for a draw-down. 'Now I'm one of them low-lifes that's about to kill you,' Allison told him. They were out at the corral and the foreman Bedford was watching them at a distance. 'So let's see what you can do about it. The surest way to be legal about it,' Allison added, 'is to let me make the first move.'

Sumner nodded.

'You're a dirty yellow coward that shot three men down in cold blood,' Allison growled out.

'Prove it,' Sumner challenged him.

Allison began a draw that had beaten other men from Texas to Missouri, his gun coming into his hand like lightning magic.

When the Colt was just leveling itself at Sumner's belly, Allison saw that Sumner's six-shooter was already aimed at his heart. He had barely seen it happen.

Allison's eyes widened in shock. He had never been beaten before.

'Good Jesus! How did you do that?'

Sumner smiled in satisfaction. He twirled the Colt backwards twice and let it nestle back into its well-oiled holster. 'You shouldn't be surprised. It's what you taught me.'

Over at the corral fence, Bedford had turned and was telling a ranch hand what he had seen. Allison had re-holstered too, and now walked over to Sumner. 'I never taught you that, boy! I never saw a draw like that. You're a by-God natural!'

'It was a lucky draw,' Sumner said. 'Next time you'll beat me.'

'Like hell I will. You've arrived, Sumner.' His face became pensive.

'I reckon that means you won't be with me much longer.'

Sumner sighed. 'I'll never forget this time with you, Clay.'

Allison grabbed him by the shoulder. 'Well, let's not get all sad-faced about it. How much longer will you stay with us?'

'Till the end of the month,' Sumner said. 'Till I get my pay.'

'That ain't hardly a week,' Allison said to himself. He was shaking his head. 'Well, tell you what. Why don't we ride into Las Animas tonight. Just you and me. And celebrate what's happened here. We'll make it a night to remember.'

'That suits me right down to the ground.' Sumner smiled.

It was just a half hour's ride into town. They arrived at the Last Chance Saloon just as darkness fell and there was already a small crowd inside. The saloon was sophisticated for the size of the town. There was a long mahogany bar, and a large painting of a reclining nude on the wall behind it. Shelves of bottles contained every kind of whiskey, rum, or any other sort of hard drink available at the time. Faro tables at the rear were already busy with customers, and a Wurlitzer piano sat closed up in a corner. A sign on the back wall announced free eggs with every beer or ale.

Allison walked in ahead of Sumner, and a couple of tables of drinkers near the door went quiet when they saw him. Most men in the area hoped Allison was in a good mood when he came to drink. At a table in the centre of the room, a tough-looking man with a three day beard took particular notice of Allison. His name was Curly Quentin and he was wanted for robbery and murder in three states. Allison spotted him too, but ignored his presence. He had never thought it his duty to concern himself about any outlaws who might ride through his area. He had committed too many unlawful acts himself.

Allison and Sumner ordered Planter's Rye and it was brought to them by a skinny waiter who sneaked a long look at Allison. Allison toasted Sumner's future with their first drink, and then said, 'Frankly, boy, I wish you wasn't headed in the direction you picked.'

Sumner's handsome face was grave. 'I don't have any choice, Clay.'

'You know you're not ready yet, don't you? Them Territory deputies are mostly notorious gunslingers themselves. And I've heard about Pritchard. He's dangerous.'

'I know all that,' Sumner assured him. 'I intend to take my time with this.'

Suddenly there was a loud yell from the centre table. 'Hey, Allison! You still wading in cow pucky for fun?' It was Quentin. The other two men at his table, a couple of grubby drifters, laughed softly. The rest of the room slowly quieted down.

Allison looked over at him. 'Are you still robbing women and babies for their cookie jar cash, Quentin?' he replied in a hard voice.

Sumner frowned. 'Is that Curly Quentin?'

Allison nodded. 'He's got the idea he's the fastest gun in five states,' he said drily. 'He's a self-made legend, you might say. But he's worth avoiding.'

Quentin swigged an ale. 'Say, Allison! Word has it you took in a damn back-shooter. Some yellow-belly called Sumner. Is that him there with you?'

The whole room had gone deadly silent now. A man at a front table got up and quietly left the saloon.

Allison sighed. 'Don't pay him no mind,' he told Sumner. 'I'll handle it. If I have to.'

Sumner shook his head. 'No. I don't want that.'

Quentin yelled again, 'That sure looks like the kind of milkweed that would bushwhack an unsuspecting victim! Don't you agree, boys?'

At a far table, a fork clinked on glass and sounded like a small cannon firing in the room.

Sumner set his shot glass down. 'You're in no danger, Quentin. You're facing me.' Slowly and deliberately.

Over at the other table, Quentin's face went straight-lined, looking even uglier. Allison turned to Sumner. 'Sumner. That's Curly Quentin. You ain't ready yet, boy.'

But Quentin was rising menacingly from his chair now. He stepped away from his table. Several men in the line of fire moved away, scraping their chairs in their haste.

'Are you saying you want to try me, yellow streak?'

Sumner had had enough. He rose and moved carefully away from his chair. Allison watching somberly but silently. Sumner looked as calm as if he were target practising.

'That's what I'm saying. Unless, of course, you'd care to disown those rude remarks you just made.'

Quentin's face turned crimson. Then, without warning, he drew.

But by the time his gun had cleared leather, Sumner's Colt appeared in his hand as if it had already been there. Its quick thunder exploded into the room as Quentin's shot roared out a split second later, the two weapons making the rafters shake. Quentin's hot lead tore at Sumner's shirt under his left arm, and Sumner's had already burst Quentin's heart like a paper bag and busted two posterior ribs as it exited his thick frame.

Quentin went flying backwards, arms flailing. His gun went off again, and bottles were smashed on the shelf near the bartender and sticky liquid sprayed onto his chest and face. Quentin crashed past two tables, taking them and chairs with him, splintering wood and spilling drinks as he hit the floor with a loud thud. Eyes staring unseeing at the tin ceiling, in the rictus of death. His left leg drummed the floor for a moment and he was lifeless.

The acrid odour of gun smoke hung in the air as Sumner casually twirled the Peacemaker over twice and into its oiled resting place.

'Holy Christ!' From the sticky bartender. Eyes wide.

'Did you see that?' In a hushed voice, from a far corner.

Sumner sat back down, picked up his shot glass and swigged its contents. 'Now. What were we saying?' In the same calm, modulated voice.

Allison let a smile cross his broad face. 'Well. Look what we done out there.'

Now the noise was returning to the room, with men talking fast and excitedly. The bartender and his waiter were bending over Quentin's corpse in preparation to taking it to a back room.

'You know who you are now?' Allison was saying to Sumner.

Sumner was assessing his feelings about what had just happened. He found that he was unmoved. He regarded Allison now curiously.

'You'll always be the man that killed Curly Quentin,' Allison said quietly.

Sumner shrugged. 'He started to get under my skin.'

Allison shook his head slowly. 'It's clear as sheet lightning under thunderheads. You ain't no ranch hand no more. You got talent, boy.'

Sumner looked sober. 'It's not something I wanted.'

The bartender appeared suddenly beside their table, wiping at his face with a bar cloth. 'Well, Sumner. You not only did this town a big favor just now. You just earned yourself $1,000.'

Sumner turned to him, frowning. 'What the hell are you talking about?'

'He means there's a bounty on that ugly boy's head,' Allison explained. 'You just made yourself some traveling cash, boy.'

Sumner was trying to digest that. 'I don't want money for killing a man,' he said quietly.

'You better take it,' the bartender quipped. 'It's just waiting there to be paid to the right man.' Then he was gone.

Allison swigged the remainder of his drink. 'You'd be a fool to let it lie, boy. This is your chance to grab yourself a real grub-stake. For what you got ahead of you eventually.'

Sumner met his look. The idea was completely alien to him. 'I'll be around a few more days. I'll give it some thought.'

Before they left town that evening, Allison persuaded him to stop at the local sheriff's office and put in his claim, just in case. A few days later, Sumner was packed up on his black stallion, and saying goodbye to Allison. The foreman Bedford was a different man toward him, offering him a sheepskin coat and treating Sumner like a celebrity.

'Where are you headed?' Allison asked him.

'I have no idea,' Sumner told him. 'I have to check up on Pritchard and Guthrie. Whether they're still at Fort Sill. I can't plan beyond that.'

'I wish I could talk you out of this,' Allison told him. 'I run into Pritchard once. He'd make Curly Quentin look like a raw greenhorn. And that partner of his is slick as oiled leather.'

'I don't have a choice in this,' Sumner said quietly. 'This is more important to me than my life.'

Allison nodded reluctantly. 'I've had that feeling. Well, you stop by here when it's over, you hear?'

Sumner smiled at him. 'I will,' he told him. Then he was gone.

It was later that same day that Sumner stopped at the sheriff's office in Las Animas and was paid out $1,000 in coin and paper by a scowling lawman.

'We don't cotton much to bounty hunters hereabouts,' was his remark when Sumner was paid. 'We'd like to see you move on, Sumner.'

Sumner gave him an acid look. 'I'm not a bounty hunter, Sheriff. I didn't kill Curly Quentin for money. But if I had, I wouldn't be apologizing to any lawman that sat around and watched Quentin tear up their towns without lifting a finger to stop him.'

Sumner left the sheriff looking after him with a worried look on his face, and walked down to the local bank and deposited most of the cash in a new account. As he left the bank, he realized that he was now a man of property, and that was a new feeling for him. He went into a dry goods store and came back out with different clothing. Dark trousers and jacket. Blue shirt and black cravat at the neck. It was all done on a rather subconscious level, but he was dressed now for a dark purpose. The ranch hand Sumner, which had never really existed as a permanent entity, was gone forever. With the black, flat-top Stetson and the black stallion, he looked like a man you might want to avoid, if you saw him ride past.

After the clothing change, he found a hardware store and purchased a deadly Hotchkiss repeating rifle which ended up in his saddle scabbard, and also a Derringer-type Harrington Pocket Pistol in a cut-down holster that fit nicely on his gun-belt at the small of his back. When he boarded the stallion again out on the street he felt he was physically ready now for the mission that lay ahead.

He felt, for the first time in his life, dangerous.

CHAPTER FOUR

The bustling town of Fort Griffin was on Sumner's route south before he crossed over into Indian Territory, and he reached it in the late afternoon of his first day out of Las Animas. He had been there as a boy, at a time when he was still looking for the men who murdered his aunt, and a storekeeper named Hawley had befriended him then and had tried to dissuade him from going after the outlaws. Sumner decided to look him up now again, because Hawley had connections in the Territory.

Sumner stopped at a small hotel called the Lone Star and was given a room by a bespectacled clerk who looked him over suspiciously. With his mount ensconced in a nearby hostelry, he then walked down to a general store where he hoped to find Hawley. The streets were busy with traffic and Sumner recalled that Fort Griffin had been, at one time, the site of an annual rendezvous where mountain men, hunters and trappers, and Indians from five or six tribes met to buy, sell and trade furs, hides, equipment and guns. Now there was just a remnant of all that in mid-summer. But the town sat on a cattle trail and had prospered well.

When Sumner walked into the general store, Hawley was behind a long counter that displayed clothing and household goods. Hawley recognized Sumner immediately.

'Well, I'll be a puffed-up horny toad! Look what we have here!'

There were no customers in the place. Hawley came around the counter and reached out and pumped Sumner's hand vigorously, looking him over openly. 'Good God! You look all growed up! And different!'

'Pleasured to see you again, Mr Hawley.' Sumner smiled at him.

Hawley was grinning. He was a middle-aged fellow with a round, pleasant face and a pot belly. 'I see you come up in the world since I seen you last.' Looking at Sumner's new attire.

'Not very far,' Sumner told him. 'You look just the same after eight or nine years.'

Hawley gave him a sly grin. 'I see you learned diplomacy, too.' He leaned against the counter. 'Word come to me that you ignored my advice, back there.' Sumner nodded. 'It had to be done. And I paid my dues.'

'You look bigger. More mature.'

Sumner sighed heavily, looking down.

'I feel more mature,' he admitted. 'Look. Do you have time for a brief sit down, Mr Hawley?'

'Hell, yes. You like a cup of Brazilian coffee?'

'If you have it.'

Hawley went and hung a 'Closed' sign on the front door, and then led Sumner to a back room where there were cooking facilities. In moments, they were sitting at a kitchen table with their coffee before them. Sumner stirred his cup pensively.

'What have you been doing with yourself, boy?' Hawley finally asked him.

'Oh, I've been doing some ranching,' Sumner said evasively.

'You don't look like no ranch hand.' Hawley grinned at him. Then his face turned somber. 'The word is that somebody named Sumner just shot and killed one of the worst hombres seen in these parts in quite a spell. The rumor is that this Sumner is blinding fast with a gun and can shoot the eye out of a jack of spades across a crowded room in the dark.'

Sumner shook his head. 'That Sumner must be some kind of phenomenon,' he responded with a wry grin.

Hawley sipped at his coffee. 'I give you the wrong advice back there when you was here before,' he said slowly. 'You had every right. And you never should have been punished for it.'

'That means a lot to me,' Sumner told him. 'Listen. I have a similar situation going on right now. And maybe you can help me. As I recall, you have some connections over in the Territory.'

'I got some acquaintances over that way.'

'You know anybody over at Fort Sill?'

'Not really. But I hear news from there pretty regular.'

'What about the federal judge over there? You hear anything about him or his deputies?'

Hawley's eyebrows shot upward. 'Oh. Didn't you know? Judge Gabriel got in big trouble with his bosses back in Washington, and he was removed from office. Just last week.'

Sumner narrowed his blue eyes. 'What?'

'I got it from a reliable source. He was called the hanging judge, as you may know.'

'I know.'

'A real bastard. Did you have trouble with him?'

Sumner looked across the room, and remembered. 'His deputies beat my friend to death. And Gabriel let it happen. He had sentenced Corey to hang. But he didn't make it to the gallows.'

'Jesus,' Hawley mumbled.

'What happened to the deputies that did his dirty work? Called Guthrie and Pritchard?'

Hawley grunted out a laugh. 'They're in worse trouble than Gabriel, I hear. They raped and damn near killed a local girl of the streets just before Gabriel was fired. Their boss, the US District Marshal, came to arrest them but they had run off somewhere. They think to Mexico.'

Sumner looked away. 'Sonofabitch.'

Hawley narrowed his eyes, too. 'What did you have in mind, boy?'

Sumner met his look with a rock-steady one. 'Payback,' he grated out.

'All of them?'

'Gabriel is probably back East in disgrace,' Sumner said pensively. 'Letting that half-man live out his life now as a pariah is punishment enough.'

'But the deputies?'

Sumner looked over at him. 'I hoped I'd find them in Fort Sill. But I will find them, Mr Hawley. If I have to chase them to China. I told them they'd pay for Corey's death. And I meant it.'

'You won't know where to start,' Hawley argued. 'They could be in Mexico City. Or Venezuela.'

Sumner shook his head. 'I don't see them as taking to exotic places. If they're in Mexico, it won't be for long. I'll start at Fort Sill. Try to get some information there. Maybe there's someone who knew them.'

Hawley sat back on his chair and sipped at his coffee. 'I know you must be good. Because Curly Quentin was good. But I've heard things about this Pritchard, Sumner. If he finds out you're after him, he'll try to come on you some black night and back-shoot you. And he'll want to make it slow for you when he kills you. And if there is a drawdown, he's deadly with a gun.'

Sumner held his gaze silently.

'And that other one, as I hear it, can draw so fast you can't see his hand go to the holster.' He paused. 'But maybe them stories is all bull-pucky.'

Sumner let a wry smile touch his lips. 'You're beginning to sound like you did nine years ago.'

'Nine years ago you wasn't going after Pritchard and Guthrie,' Hawley said quietly.

Sumner set his cup down. 'Maybe nobody else can understand this. That boy was the first friend I'd made in ten years, and the only one in my adult life. I planned to mentor him, bring him along. That kid was raw innocence, he was beginning to feel like a younger brother to me. I had to tell his sister what had happened to him.'

'He had a sister?'

'Jane. A sweet girl.' He looked off beyond Hawley.

'Sounds like she made an impression on you.'

'I liked her. I liked her a lot.'

Hawley regarded him seriously. 'Too bad about this other thing.'

Sumner looked back at him.

77

'I mean, the girl. You might have made something of that.'

Sumner grunted. 'I'm aware of that.'

'So this dislike of them two wins out over what you feel for his sister.'

Sumner squinted down on him. 'Dislike? I still haven't made myself clear, it seems. This thing they did to Corey eats at my insides, Mr Hawley. Day and night. Like acid in there. If those two got away with what they did, this world would become Hades itself to me. I don't want to live in a world where that can happen and not be answered. And there's nobody to answer it but me.'

Hawley sighed. 'Then I guess it's like before. You have to do it.'

'That's the way I figure it. And it's for Jane, too.'

Hawley smiled. 'Is that the way she sees it?'

Sumner met his look, but did not respond.

'It's for you, boy. Don't put it on nobody else. Let's just hope it don't turn around and bite you on the butt. Even if everything goes like you hope.'

'Jane?'

'That's your likely future, ain't it? If this works out for you?'

Sumner rose from his chair. 'You're too many chess moves ahead, Mr Hawley. My future is right now.'

Hawley rose, too. 'Go carefully, Sumner. And keep your cartridge belt filled.'

'That's my plan,' Sumner told him.

Before he left town that afternoon, Sumner stopped briefly at a local bank and obtained help from a bank officer to make out a last will and testament. He figured it was important now that he had some property and because of what he was headed into. He left all of his worldly belongings and property to Jane Madison, and then mailed it to her at Blaneyville.

By late afternoon he was on his way to Fort Sill.

After a long ride through arid back country that day, Sumner arrived at a small crossroads village called Apache Junction just a short time before dark. It was one of those end-of-the-world backwater towns with hot, dusty streets and unpainted clapboard buildings surrounding a central plaza. There was a city hall, a general store and a saloon. A two storey boarding house crouched at the end of the street.

Sumner reined in at the Trail's End Saloon and found it almost deserted at that time of day. There was a brawny bartender, and a table where three men were playing One-Eyed Jacks. There was sawdust on the rived-plank floor, and a sign on a back wall that read, *All Hard Drinks 25c. Ice 5c Extra.*

Sumner stepped up to the bar and ordered a dark ale, glancing toward the card players. When the barkeep arrived with Sumner's drink, Sumner spoke to him.

'Would that boarding house down the street be a hazard to my health?'

'Oh. You heard about the bedbugs. No, that's all been cleaned up. You could rent them rooms in Austin.'

Sumner gave him a distasteful look. 'Appreciate the recommendation.'

The barkeep looked him over. 'Say, are you a gambler, mister?'

'Can't say I am.'

'I wouldn't ask you your name.'

Sumner took a drink of the ale. 'It's Sumner. Wesley Sumner.'

The bartender's eyes widened, and the men at the table stopped what they were doing and stared over at Sumner.

'You're Sumner?' the barkeep said soberly.

Sumner frowned at him. 'Is that a problem?'

'No, no!' the other man replied. 'Are you the Sumner that killed Curly Quentin?'

Sumner's frown deepened. He set his glass down. 'Are you writing a book or something, mister?'

The barkeep forced a tight grin on. 'Sorry, Sumner. Don't pay me no mind. Sometimes I get just as brash as a flour peddler running for governor. I don't mean nothing by it.'

Over at the card table, one of the players tapered up a cigarette, and a second one, a big brawny fellow, turned to the others and made some remarks in a low voice.

The bartender was leaning toward Sumner now. 'Say, you know the outlaw Joaquin Murrieta? I got his head in the back room, pickled in a jar of alcohol. Some drummer left it here temporarily. I been charging customers a dollar to see it, but I'd let you take a look for free.'

Sumner shook his head. 'Why don't you go wash some glasses?'

The barkeep nodded. 'Yes, sir. No offense.'

When he was gone, Sumner sipped at the ale and remembered. That day at the Madison farm when he and Corey were just out of prison, and he first met Jane, and how her first smile at him had raised his blood pressure. You just didn't find a girl that good-looking and still single. He had felt something for her at first sight. Then, when he had returned without her brother and had had to tell her what happened, it tore him up inside to see what that did to her. If he survived Pritchard and Guthrie, he knew he had to go back there. To see if she still gave him that lovely smile when she saw him.

'Hey, mister!' From the table behind him.

Sumner turned with his drink in hand, and saw it was the brawny man who had called out to him.

'Are you talking to me?'

'Yeah, I'm talking to you,' the brawny fellow replied. 'Are you passing yourself off as that Sumner boy? The one that murdered Quentin?'

'I'm not passing myself off,' Sumner told him. He finished the ale. 'I'm Wesley Sumner. If that's any of your business.'

The third man at the table, wearing ranch hand clothes, leaned toward his brawny companion. 'Why don't you let it go, Gus. If that's Sumner, he killed Curly Quentin in a fair draw-down. And Quentin was good.'

'Shut up, Wylie,' Gus growled at him.

The one who had lit up a cigarette threw some cards onto the table and rose from his chair. Gus looked over at him.

'I ain't staying for this,' the fellow responded. 'I got a bad feeling about it.'

'There ain't nothing happening I can't handle,' Gus growled out. 'Set down and relax.'

But his companion wasn't listening. 'I'll see you back at the ranch.' Then he gave Sumner a quick glance and left the saloon. The other cohort, Wylie, ran a hand across his mouth, looking skittery as a turkey trapped in a wire pen with a rattler.

But Gus was in a mood for trouble. 'If you're really that Sumner,' he called out to Sumner, 'the one that shot Quentin, I hear you didn't give him a chance. That it was just yellow-belly murder.'

Sumner shook his head, and turned back to the bar. The barkeep was still standing nearby, trying to hold his breath through this. 'Barman, I'll try a glass of your Red Top Rye.'

'We don't have the Red Top,' was the answer. Dry-mouthed. 'I can give you the Planter's Rye.'

'All right, the Planter's. But don't water it down so it tastes like cow piss.'

'Yes, sir. I think you'll like it, all right. Can I get you a boiled egg or a calf sandwich?'

'Just the rye,' Sumner told him.

'Hey, Sumner! Did you hear what I said about Quentin?'

Sumner ignored him.

'Come on, Gus. Let it go.' From his partner.

'I asked you a question, mister. And people usually answer me when I talk to them.'

The bartender nervously delivered Sumner's drink. 'I don't want no trouble in here.' In a hushed tone.

'Tell Gus,' Sumner said quietly. Then he swigged the rye whiskey in one gulp.

'What's the matter, hot shot?' Gus went on. He wore a Schofield .45 revolver very low on his hip, and it stuck out menacingly in bold view at the moment. 'Afraid to talk about it?'

'Why don't you check out that boarding house we talked about?' the bartender said to Sumner a bit breathlessly. 'Think you'll like the proprietor. She once shook hands with Jesse James.'

'I intend to walk on down there,' Sumner told him. 'After this flea-brain quits yelling at me.'

Gus heard the remark, and scraped his chair away from the table. 'What did you say about me?' In a lower tone now. 'I won't stand for no saucy manner, back-shooter.'

Sumner turned to face him. Like Curly Quentin before him, Gus had finally gotten into Sumner's craw. 'Boy, you don't know when to quit. If your brains were dynamite, you couldn't blow the top of your head off.'

Gus's face crimsoned, and he rose from his chair and stepped away from the table. He scowled fiercely at Sumner now, his eyes the color of granite. 'That does it!' he rasped out. 'Defend yourself, you goddamn dandy!'

'Gus,' his partner protested quietly from his chair.

Sumner sighed and stepped reluctantly away from the bar, squaring away with the other man. He didn't need this. His only thoughts now were on the two Territory deputies.

'All right. If you insist.'

Gus was beyond restraint. He hesitated for just a moment. Then he drew the Schofield in a sudden movement.

Sumner, though, had read his intent in his eyes before Gus had made a move to his holster. As Gus's revolver cleared leather, Sumner's Colt appeared magically in his right hand so fast there was no time for the movement to register in Gus's head, or recall that Sumner's hand had gone to his hip.

Gus's gun was out and clear to fire, but he hadn't had time to aim it, as he saw Sumner's gun trained directly on his heart. He was beaten badly, and in that moment in eternity, his beefy face changed expression, a look of cold fear possessing it. He knew he was a dead man.

And in that split second of heavy, timeless silence, Sumner's Colt began erupting into a deafening roar, ripping the close air like repeating thunderbolts, with Sumner in a half-crouch, fanning the Colt's hammer.

In less than two seconds, hot lead struck Gus's gun hand and tore the Schofield from his grasp, sending it flying across the room, then cut Gus's holster loose from his gun-belt, making it clatter to the floor. And in a last second, a third blast from the Colt struck the chain of a glass chandelier hanging over the card table, severed it, and sent the whole apparatus plunging down onto Gus's head and shoulders, taking Gus with it as it crashed to the hardwood floor. The table went, too, leaving Wylie on his isolated chair. Stunned.

Gun smoke was so thick Wylie tasted it on his tongue.

Sumner rose from the crouch as the bartender uttered a low whistle between his teeth. 'I never seen nothing like that in all my born days.' In a half whisper.

Gus's companion raised his hands. 'For God's sake, don't shoot! Don't kill me!'

Sumner twirled the deadly-looking Colt Peacemaker in a dazzling display and returned it home.

'I didn't kill this loud-mouth, did I?' Sumner said casually. Looking as cool and collected as he had been before it all happened. The fellow called Wylie eased off his chair, made a wide circuit around Sumner, and left the saloon. Sumner turned from the debris-littered figure on the floor to the bartender.

'Now. Let's talk about that flea-bag down the street.'

CHAPTER FIVE

After the brief stop at Apache Junction, Sumner rode hard for two days and arrived in Fort Sill on an overcast afternoon. He rode slowly to the town square, remembering being brought there handcuffed by their captors. When he arrived at the central square, he reined in and stared somberly at the scene before him. There was the court house and jail building, where he and Corey had been jailed and tried. And standing ominously before the building was the gallows where they would have hanged Corey if he had survived the beating.

It was a very emotional moment for Sumner. The stallion shuffled under him, wondering why they were motionless. Sumner patted it on its dark neck.

'You wouldn't understand,' he said softly to his mount.

He finally rode on up to the brick building and tethered the horse there. Memories came flashing at him like bats in a cave. He stood there a long moment, then went into the building.

The main floor consisted of offices and, at the rear, the jail cells where he and Corey had spent a brief time together. The second floor was taken up mostly by the court room where Judge Gabriel had handed down his deadly decrees. And also Gabriel's private chambers, and another office, for the bailiff and court clerk.

There was nobody in sight when he entered. He walked down the corridor to the cells, and looked into the one where they had kept him and Corey. He felt something grab at his insides as he stood there. After a long moment he returned to the front. A young man emerged from an office and stared at him.

'You looking for somebody?'

'Yes. But they're not here now.'

The fellow gave him a look of curiosity. Staring at Sumner's dark clothing. 'You look familiar. Were you a deputy here?'

'No. I was a prisoner,' Sumner answered him.

The other man's face quickly became serious. 'I see.'

'No, you don't,' Sumner told him. 'I hear they sent the district marshal over here. Is he around somewhere?'

The other man looked Sumner over again. 'Not at the moment. But we expect him shortly. I can tell him you want to see him, if you don't want to wait.'

'I'll be back,' Sumner told him.

'Shall I tell him who wants to see him?'

'No.' Then he turned and left the building.

Outside under threatening thunderheads, Sumner mounted the black stallion again, and rode out to the north edge of town, where he found the local cemetery, which the locals called Boot Hill. He picketed his horse and made his way to what appeared to be the newer part of the cemetery. After a brief search, he found a grave site where grass had not yet grown back. On the site a wooden cross had been planted into the ground, and a name had been awkwardly inscribed on it in black paint, probably by a grave-digger. It said simply: *C. Maddison* in crooked print.

Sumner knelt on one knee. 'They couldn't even bother to spell your name right.' He felt somehow calmer inside, just being so close again to what was left of his friend.

He had picked a yellow wildflower on his way in, and now shoved its roots into the ground before Corey's cross. 'You know what I'm going to do. It's what you'd do if you could. What you'd do for me. And I know you won't rest easy till it's done. So my path is clear.'

He rose to his feet. 'I saw Jane, Corey, and she knows. I'm hoping to go back there. You know why. When this is all over.' He paused. 'I'll be back. If it goes well.'

When he left the cemetery, Sumner felt just a little better inside about what lay before him. He knew it was something Corey would want. Maybe even demand.

When he arrived back at the courthouse after an hour had passed, he went inside and found the marshal's office, and the marshal was there. A young female clerk ushered him into the marshal's private office, one he usually visited irregularly as he rode a circuit. He looked up with a frown when Sumner entered.

'Who the hell are you?'

He was a large man, at over six feet, and chunky in his dress clothes and lariat tie. He was in his forties, with a square, lined face, and looked as hard as sacked salt.

'I'm Wesley Sumner. I understand you worked this area under Judge Gabriel.'

'Not under Gabriel. With Gabriel. And like I said, who are you?'

'Do you mind if I sit?'

'Suit yourself.' He sat back on a high-backed chair and clasped his hands behind his head.

Sumner took a chair not far from the desk the marshal occupied. He was wearing his dark jacket, but it was open and the Colt Peacemaker stood out boldly from behind it. 'I was here a while back. As a prisoner.'

The marshal's eyebrows shot upward.

'I was innocent, and even that piece of slime Hezekiah Gabriel couldn't find any evidence to hang me.'

'You're talking about a goddamn federal judge here, Mr Sumner.'

'I know that. And he wasn't fit to clean the toilets here.'

A frown developed on the marshal's face. 'You got a foul mouth on you, boy.' He brought his hands forward, and leaned onto his desk. 'I know what Gabriel was. Is. And I know I could have done something about it, and didn't. He won't never work in the system again. But if he released you, what's got the bile worked up in you?'

Sumner looked toward a window. 'He let two of his deputies beat my friend to death. It's them I'm interested in.'

'Pritchard and Guthrie?'

Sumner grunted. 'The same.'

'There's a warrant out for their arrest. They'll be brought back to me and a new judge will try and hang them.'

'No, they won't,' Sumner said.

The marshal, whose name was Atkins, screwed his thick face up questioningly. 'Who says?'

'I say,' Sumner said easily. 'You have no deputies now.

89

And by the time you manage to hire a couple, there will be cases to solve right here in the Territory. And if you did send them out, it might be a year before they found those two. During which you'd be right where you are now. I don't really think your political bosses would put up with that. So that's why I say they won't be brought back here to hang.'

Atkins looked over toward a window on the square, where the gallows stood. 'I see you got this all thought out.'

'I've given it some thought.'

The marshal narrowed his eyes at Sumner. 'How come you speak so well, son? You go to one of them back-East colleges?'

Sumner smiled. 'I spent some years in prison. I read almost every day. My aunt used to tell me nothing was more important.'

Atkins nodded. 'I wish I'd had an aunt like that. I seen your case file here. You're from Texas, right?'

'I am.'

'Is that where you did your time?'

'That's right, Marshal. I murdered three men. They had killed my aunt.'

Atkins let a slow smile take over his face. Then it faded. 'You're going after them boys.'

'Somebody has to.'

'Are you a bounty hunter?'

'I'm not.'

'We put bounties on them two,' Atkins said.

'It doesn't interest me.'

'So it's just revenge. For your friend. And maybe yourself.'

'It's the pursuit of justice,' Sumner told him.

'But this happened a year ago. Why now?'

'I wasn't ready till now. Physically or mentally.'

'You do a lot of thinking, don't you, boy?'

Sumner sighed. 'I was hoping you could give me some information about them. Where they might have headed, and why.'

The marshal blew his cheeks out. 'I can't collude with a vigilante, son. I'd be breaking about ten commandments of my job.'

'I'm just a citizen you're sitting here jawing with,' Sumner argued. 'You don't really know what I'd do with information on them.'

Atkins grinned slightly. 'You'd make a pretty damn good lawyer, boy.' He sat there thinking. 'I personally have no idea where them low-lifes would run off to. Gabriel told the authorities Mexico, but I don't buy that. Neither one can speak a word of Spanish. But there is this fellow lives across town here. A drunken sop. But he had some inherited money, and he bought them two drinks all the time. I was about to go pay him a visit myself.'

'What's his name?' Sumner asked.

'You going to try to beat me there?'

'Face reality, Marshal. What can you do with anything he'd tell you?'

Atkins sighed rather heavily. 'I should just throw you out of here.' He paused. 'But I guess I like your grit. I'm guessing you'd stick with this till hell freezes over and then skate around on the ice for a spell before you give it up.'

Sumner grunted out his agreement. 'You got me

91

pegged, I reckon.'

'Well. His name is Cinch Bug Suggs. Nobody knows his real first name. Lives in a shanty out on the Tulsa road. But I want to go with you.'

Sumner hesitated. 'All right.'

It was a short ride out to Suggs's cabin. It sat on a busy stage trail, and its façade was covered with trail dust, including the glass in the two windows. They left the mounts at a dilapidated hitching post and pounded on the heavy pine door with its leather hinges. After a long moment, a skinny, disheveled man opened the door and stared at them blankly, squinting in the dull sun. His stringy hair hung into his face, and his nose was broken.

'Are you Suggs?' the marshal demanded.

Suggs saw the star on Atkins's vest. 'The law? I didn't do it, Marshal!! I swear to God!'

'Didn't do what?' Atkins growled at him.

'Nothing! Whatever it is, I'm innocent! I'll swear on a Bible! Get me a Bible, Marshal, and I'll swear to God on it!'

Atkins made a face. 'We'd like to talk to you, Suggs. Can we come in for a few minutes?'

Suggs hesitated, then nodded vigorously. 'Sure. You can come in. I got nothing in there you can't see. And I wasn't at the saloon Tuesday night when that fellow was knocked down, Marshal. I was right here drinking my own liquor.'

'Just relax, Suggs,' Atkins told him. At just over six feet, about Sumner's height, he towered over Suggs.

Sumner and the marshal looked around the one room cabin. There was an old fireplace on one wall, and across from it was an unmade bunk. There was a table and two straight chairs in the centre of the room, with two half-full whiskey bottles on it, and on a back wall were shelves that held some cans and jars of food. The floor was littered with scraps of paper and stained with dried spills of various kinds.

'Won't you boys have a seat?' Suggs said, pushing hair off his forehead. He grabbed the two bottles and deposited them on a foot locker at the end of the bunk. 'I'd offer you coffee, but I ain't got a fire.'

'We're all right,' Atkins told him. The two of them seated themselves at the table, and Suggs stood near them.

'We understand you knew Duke Pritchard and Maynard Guthrie,' Atkins said.

Suggs swallowed hard. 'I wasn't with them when they went to that Kruzick girl. I was here. I got witnesses.'

'We know that,' Atkins said sharply. 'Listen to me. When them two rode out of here, did they talk to you?'

Suggs licked dry lips. 'I might have saw them the day before they left.'

'What did you talk about?'

'Well. You know, they'd heard you was going to arrest them.'

'And they decided to run,' Sumner put in.

Suggs looked over at him. 'Are you a new deputy?'

'I asked you a question, goddamn it,' Sumner spat out.

The marshal glanced over at him. 'Well, let's give Mr Suggs a chance to remember that moment,' he said meaningfully. 'They told you they had to get out of town. Is that right?'

Suggs sneaked a quick peek at Sumner. 'That's right.'

'Where did they say they were headed?' Atkins said.

Suggs looked from him to Sumner and back. 'They was pretty vague about where they was headed. Seems like I heard something about Mexico.'

'That's bull-pucky,' Sumner grated out.

Suggs gave Sumner a scared look. 'Well, it might be. But that's all I know about it. They didn't really tell me much, you know.' He looked quickly at the floor.

'Well, now look here, Suggs. . .' the marshal began.

But Sumner had gotten to his feet, and now he stepped over to Suggs and casually drew the Peacemaker and snugged it up against Suggs's chest.

'Now, you lying sonofabitch. Tell us where they rode off to, or I'm going to blow your liver out through your greasy back.' In a low, menacing tone.

'Sumner,' came Atkins's cautious voice.

But Suggs believed Sumner. His tongue clicked now on a paper-dry mouth. 'OK. They didn't talk about Mexico. Except to send you off in a wrong direction.'

'Where then?' Sumner persisted.

Suggs glanced at Atkins as if for protection. 'Guthrie's got this old drinking friend up in Kansas. Dodge City, maybe. I think they was headed there.'

'If you're lying to me, I'll be back,' Sumner told him.

Suggs shook his head. 'I ain't lying.'

Sumner put the gun away. Suggs was breathing shallowly. 'Well, we appreciate your cooperation, Suggs,' Atkins told him, giving Sumner a hard look. He turned to leave and Sumner followed him to the door.

'Nice place you got here,' Sumner said as they left.

Outside, when they arrived at their mounts, Atkins leaned on his animal's flank and glared at Sumner. 'I should arrest you for what you done in there. I'm the by-God law around here, goddamn it, and I got rules to live by.'

'Tell that to your deputies,' Sumner suggested. 'Anyway, you didn't use any persuasion. I did.'

Atkins stood there staring at Sumner. 'That pleasant face of yours hides a lot of hostility, son. You're too young to have such a dark view of the world.'

'The world put it there,' Sumner told him.

'If you're not careful, it could put you six feet under.'

Sumner grunted. 'I reckon we'll have to see how it all plays out.'

'You know, Kansas is a pretty wild place right now. Maybe even more so than the Territory.'

'That's probably why they headed there.'

'There's winds of change sweeping across the West. Since the Dry Laws were passed in Kansas and other places, every psalm-singing nut from back East claims a licence to come in and close down saloons and liquor stores and build their churches and meeting halls. Wichita and Dodge City have been two of their target towns, and it's caused big trouble. The saloons have hired professional gunslingers to keep the prohibitionists at bay, and now there are guns on the other side. In Dodge they're calling it the Dodge City War. There have been a few casualties. You could be riding into a firestorm.'

'I don't care where this takes me.'

'There's no guarantee they'll even be in Kansas,' Atkins suggested. 'That might have been another ploy to throw us off.'

'Well, that's all I have to guide me,' Sumner said. 'I figure they probably rode up north from here and crossed into Kansas around Camp Supply. I'll check there and other places along the way.'

'Tell you what. If I send a wire off to Washington I could probably get permission to join you. They're basically our problem, after all. I could get a response in a couple weeks.'

'No, thanks,' Sumner said. 'I don't have two weeks. And this isn't basically your problem. It's mine.'

'You're a stubborn sonofabitch,' Atkins said.

'I've been told that.'

'I could arrest you and keep you here till I'm ready to go,' Atkins advised him.

Sumner smiled slightly. 'Make your play, Marshal.'

'You stubborn bastard,' Atkins grumbled. He boarded his mount and Sumner followed suit.

'Come on back to town. I can give you the names of a couple settlements between here and Camp Supply. There's no stage trail in that direction.'

Sumner smiled at that. 'You're a good old boy, Marshal.'

At Atkins's invitation, Sumner slept that night in a room off the judge's chambers with a cot in it. He was gone at dawn the following morning without seeing Atkins again, and glad to be away from the place that had such bad memories for him. The weather was warming as summer approached and he now rode without his jacket and the Derringer at his back. He had, however, purchased a dark vest that gave him the look of a gambler.

By noon that day he had come to a cluster of buildings and houses situated near a creek that Atkins had told him about, which had been named Noon Tank. It consisted of a general store and saloon in one building, a blacksmith shop and six clapboard houses. There was no street, and no one visible outside as he reined in at the store and dismounted. He mounted three steps to the store and went inside. No one was there.

'Hallo, the store!' he called out, looking around. There was a counter against a back wall, behind which were shelves of clothing and ranch supplies. After a long moment, an old man appeared from a doorway to the saloon, pulling on a pair of red suspenders.

He squinted down on Sumner. 'Well, by Jesus. Where'd you come from?'

'I just rode in from Fort Sill,' Sumner said. He removed his black Stetson and wiped at his forehead. His dark hair was damp. 'You got a good bedroll in all those dry goods behind you there?'

The proprietor nodded. 'I might have one in the store-room somewhere. Thinking of making hardship camp out there, mister?' There was no response. 'I'll make sure there's a groundsheet with it.'

'Much obliged. You also have a dark ale for me in the other room?' The other man grinned, and there was a tooth missing in the front of his mouth. 'I got the best damn ale in a fifty mile range! I'll fix you up soon as I go get that bedroll.'

'Before you go,' Sumner stopped him.

The old fellow turned back to him. 'Yes, sir?'

'There are two men that might have come through here not long ago. Riding together. A big, broad-shouldered man with a scar over his right eye, and his partner is slimmer with cold grey eyes. They both wear Colt Army revolvers low on their belts.'

The proprietor rubbed his chin. 'They sound familiar.

Let me ask Lenny.' He disappeared into the saloon, and returned momentarily.

'Sure, Lenny remembers them. A couple of real ornery boys.' He grinned. 'That brawny one was brash as a camp cook doing brain surgery.' A small cackle. 'I remember them now. I wouldn't want to be the one to say no to them.'

Sumner nodded, and let out a long breath. 'How long ago was that?'

'Oh, about a week ago, I'd guess. I just took them for a couple of greasy drifters.'

'They weren't wearing badges?'

The other man's face exploded in surprise. 'Badges? God, no! They wasn't the law, was they?'

'Not now,' Sumner said pensively.

'I didn't take them for preachers. But the law! We don't never see the law here.'

'Did they mention where they were going?'

'I don't think so. They emptied one of my bottles of rum, and cleaned me out of my boiled eggs. They was like hogs rooting in a slop bucket!'

Sumner gave him a sober look. 'They`re very dangerous men. Consider yourself lucky they left without trouble. Now I'll just get myself a taste of that ale while you fetch the bedroll.'

'Coming right up,' the old fellow said brightly. 'Say, are you going after them two?'

Sumner eyed him narrowly. 'Why don't you let me ask the questions.'

A shrug. 'I just didn't see no badge.'

'I don't need one,' Sumner said. Then he went into the saloon.

He was there less than an hour. Then he was on his way again, with the black stallion rested. He rode all that afternoon through dry country dotted with huisache, jumping cholla and catclaw. In mid-afternoon he reached Camp Supply, which wasn't much bigger than Noon Tank. After a brief inquiry about Pritchard and Guthrie in a small saloon there, where nobody remembered them, Sumner decided it was too early to stop for the day, and rode on until dusk, just at the Territory border. He made hardship camp under a mesquite tree not far from a small stream.

Sumner watered the stallion at the stream and filled a canteen he kept on the horse's irons. Then he gathered some firewood, started a low fire, and put the bedroll down near the fire. He had bought a tin of beans at the store earlier, and now heated that over the fire, sitting on his saddle. Imagining what it might be like when he actually saw the two deputies again.

The fire crackled and spat at him and sent yellow fireflies of sparks into the new blackness, and Sumner found himself thinking it might be a fairly acceptable world after all, without those two in it.

As he sat there eating from the can of beans later, he stopped for a moment and listened. Yes, it was the sound of hoof beats approaching. There was no other sound quite like it. In a moment, a man on horseback appeared at the edge of Sumner's camp.

Sumner set the can down carefully and rose. Every meeting with another person on the trail was potentially dangerous. The rider came on in a few feet, and stopped in the light of the fire.

'Evening, stranger.'

He was a rather short, dumpy-looking man in dark clothing and a bowler hat. A large, black carrying case hung on his mount's flank. Sumner just watched him.

'I hope I'm not disturbing you. My name is R.C. Funk, and I travel this Godless country to try to save lost souls from spending eternity in the Fiery Place.'

'You're a Bible drummer?' Sumner said slowly, looking him over.

'Yes, I spread the word of our Lord and Savior through the greatest book ever written by the hand of man,' Funk replied with a patronizing smile. 'May I share your fire for a brief time, good sir?'

Sumner sighed. 'I can give you a cup of coffee.'

'Excellent!' He clumsily climbed off his mare appaloosa. 'If a brother or a sister is in a naked state and lacking the food sufficient for the day, yet one of you says to them, "Go in peace, keep warm and eat well", but you do not give them the necessities for their body, of what benefit is it?" James, chapter two, verse sixteen.'

'Here. Try this,' Sumner said, handing him a cup of coffee. 'Sorry I can't offer you a stool.'

'Pay it no mind.' Funk smiled. 'Blessed are the poor, for they shall inherit the earth.'

Sumner gave him an impatient look. They stood across the fire from each other, Sumner dipping into his can of beans and Funk sipping at the coffee.

'This is good. I often have to drink the chicory kind, on the trail. Are you a God-fearing man, Mister. . . .'

'Sumner.'

'Mr Sumner. I'll wager you could benefit from the purchase of one of my Bibles, sir. They go for just one dollar this spring. It's a value you'll never find in a general store.'

'I think I'll pass,' Sumner told him. 'Where do you come from?'

'Two days ago I was in Wichita,' Funk said. 'It's a lawless world in Kansas, Mr Sumner.'

'You been in Dodge?'

'No, I was told to avoid that den of iniquity. Even the prohibitionists can't seem to tame it. Are you headed there?'

'I might ride through there.'

'The Devil has the locals by the throat there, Mr Sumner. I'd advise riding around it.' He studied Sumner for a moment and repeated his question. 'Are you a man of God, sir?'

Sumner threw the bean can to the ground. 'Never thought much about it. If I did, maybe I'd wonder why He just sits up there somewhere watching all of this, and doesn't lift a finger, so to speak, to do something about it.'

'I see you're a man with his own ideas.' In a different voice. 'Would you mind if I pulled a Book out to read you a verse?'

Sumner sighed. 'You're wasting your time on a sinner, Funk. But I'll give you time for that. Then I'll be making up my bedroll.'

'I'll be just a minute,' Funk told him. 'Who knows, it might save your immortal soul.'

Sumner shook his head and stepped away to get another piece of kindling for the fire, while Funk reached into a saddle bag. When Sumner turned back with the wood, Funk had a Joslyn .44 revolver aimed at his chest.

'What the hell!' Sumner muttered. He had been relaxed about Funk because he didn't wear a gun-belt.

Funk looked different now. The pleasant smile was gone. 'Sorry to disappoint you, Sumner. But I just can't seem to find a Good Book in there.'

Sumner dropped the firewood. 'What happened to the word of God, and doing good for your neighbour?'

Funk grinned. 'Nice little show, huh? I been thinking of going on the stage with it.'

'I take it there's no Bibles in that case.'

'Never found no need for them. It never goes that far. A couple of memorized quotes. A pleasant smile. That usually does it.'

'Well. A Godless man in a Godless country. You fit right in, Funk. If that's your name.'

Funk shrugged. 'I have no apologies to make. I'm a common thief, Mr Sumner. I have to make myself a living. And this works for me.'

'And what happens after you've robbed me?' Sumner said caustically.

Funk sighed. 'That's the hard part. I'm not a stone killer. I'd like to let you walk away from this. The law goes after killers. So as you can understand, I'll expect your close cooperation. For your sake.'

'I wouldn't want to inconvenience you,' Sumner said acidly.

'Now, down to business. I've been coveting that Colt of yours ever since arrival at your camp. I won't ask you to throw it into the sand. I'd like for you to take it slowly from your holster. Very slowly. Then hand it to me muzzle toward you. The slightest misstep on your part will cause this Joslyn to blow a hole clear through you.

Otherwise, I'll have you clear out your saddle bags and pockets. If you behave the way I expect, what I'll do is tie you up and just ride out. Wouldn't that be a nice conclusion to our little adventure together?'

Sumner didn't know if that summary was an additional ploy. It seemed not, since Funk could have fired as soon as Sumner turned back toward him. But he might want Sumner alive just to do the work of turning over his valuables. Sumner made his decision and reached slowly for the Colt, with the Joslyn aimed directly at his heart. He followed directions, bringing the long revolver up very slowly, and turning it over so the muzzle faced him.

'OK?' he said.

'Nicely done,' Funk congratulated him. 'Now. Step over here and hand it to me just as it is.'

'I won't give you any trouble,' Sumner said, moving over to confront him. 'You can have the Colt and anything I have in the bags. I'm not rich, but there's some cash in the close one.'

'Excellent!' Funk grinned. He reached for the Colt. The Joslyn carefully trained on Sumner's chest.

Sumner reached the Colt out for the transfer, but as Funk started to take it, and just before it was in his grasp, Sumner turned the gun backwards just once until the muzzle was suddenly staring at Funk, and he squeezed off one quick shot.

Both guns banged out loudly in their ears, Funk's Joslyn firing a full second after the Colt. The Colt's lead blasted a blue hole in the centre of Funk's forehead and then his interrupted shot tore at Sumner's side under his vest.

Funk's eyes were staring past Sumner then, his brain

trying to understand what had happened. He took three steps backward and fell against his appaloosa, making the horse whinny softly, and then slid to the ground. His jaw worked for a moment there as if trying to forestall what had already happened. Then he was quite lifeless.

Sumner still held the Peacemaker in his right hand. He felt under his vest, and there was blood, but not much. The wound was very shallow.

He turned the Colt over again, and into its holster. Without giving Funk's corpse another look, he returned to the fire, sat back down, and poured himself a second cup of coffee.

'I should have asked how far it is to Dodge,' he said pensively.

CHAPTER SIX

The next morning Sumner crossed over into Kansas.

The countryside was changing. There was the beginning of grasslands, and he rode through long sections of wooded landscape, with aspens, cottonwoods and even birches dominating the terrain. In the afternoon he rode into a town called Sulphur Creek. He was still almost a two days' ride from Dodge City, he figured.

It was a peaceful-looking town, with wide streets lined by stores, a small hotel, and a couple of saloons. At the near end of town was a hostelry and a building that housed the town marshal's office and the jail. Not far from that was a house with a shingle outside on a post that advertised the place belonged to a veterinarian doctor.

Sumner stopped there and knocked, met at the door by a small man in spectacles. 'I'm the vet here.' He looked past him to the stallion. 'Is your horse lame?'

Sumner shook his head. 'I got a flesh wound I want bandaged, and I reckon there's no real doctor in town.'

The other man frowned. 'I'm a real doctor, mister.

Name of Scott.' He looked Sumner over, and saw the dark spot on his vest. 'Come on in, mister. I'll have a look at that.'

Sumner followed him into an examination room where there was the odor of ammonia and animals. He sat on the edge of a metal table and removed his vest and shirt and Scott came over with some alcohol and swabs. There was a three inch long, pencil-thick cut just along Sumner's lower ribs that was starting to scab over, but still bleeding onto his side.

'It's not bad. You won't even feel it in a couple days.'

'Just put something over it, Doc, and I'm out of here.'

The vet cleaned and bandaged the wound, taking his time. 'What about the other fellow?' he asked with a small grin.

'Oh, the other one won't need a doctor,' Sumner said noncommittally.

Scott read his eyes and understood. 'You know, I'm supposed to report things like this.'

'Do what you have to. But this didn't happen in this jurisdiction.'

'The Territory?'

'That's right.'

'I don't mean to throw mud on nobody's home ground, but I hear that only outlaws and loonies end up in the Territory.'

'You got it about right,' Sumner told him. 'But I'm not from there. I hail from Texas.'

The vet's face brightened. 'Well, I'll be a black-eyed rattler! What part of that sovereign state, boy?'

Sumner was buttoning his shirt back up. 'Down south. West of Austin. I lived with an aunt for a while there.'

Scott frowned slightly, 'Say, what's your name, son?'

Sumner gave him a look. Folks kept asking him to identify himself, and that might be dangerous as he closed in on his quarry. 'It's Sumner,' he said reluctantly.

The other man was standing in front of him, putting some gauze back into a small box. He stopped what he was doing. 'Wesley Sumner?' he asked in a low, hesitant voice.

Sumner frowned. 'What's that to you?' Belligerently.

Scott stepped away and sat down heavily onto a stool behind him. 'Good God!'

Sumner slipped his vest on, irritated now. 'What the hell's the matter with you?'

'You're the nephew of Rachel Sumner.'

Sumner was fully dressed again. He rose off the table, curiosity replacing the frustration in his square face, 'You knew my aunt?'

Scott looked up at him. 'Not long after your uncle passed away, I went by one day and she gave me coffee. We were both lonely people. This was maybe a year before you came to her. We had some good times. But then I was called away on a long trail drive, tending critters. Never saw Rachel again. It was over a year after – well, after she was gone that I heard what had happened.'

Dark memories and emotions swept through Sumner's head and body like a blue norther. He leaned against the table.

'It hit me hard for a while. I didn't know about you till later, and what you done. Sorry.'

'You're one of just a few who have ever expressed sympathy,' Sumner told him. 'So you knew Aunt Rachel well?'

Scott looked away. 'For a short time we were very close. I miss her still.'

Sumner suddenly felt a closeness to this animal doctor in this remote corner of Kansas that he hadn't felt since Corey Madison's death. 'I'm real glad I happened on you, Dr Scott,' he said solemnly.

'We share a deep and abiding pain,' Scott said quietly. He glanced at the revolver on Sumner's hip. 'You wear a pretty impressive piece of iron, boy. Like something you got big plans for.'

'I'm running down a couple of demons from hell,' Sumner said deliberately. 'When that's over, I won't need the gun anymore.'

'I wish I could help you.'

'They might have come through here. I was going to stop at the marshal's office. Do you think he would be there if I rode past?'

'He's usually there. Or his deputy.'

'I'll go past on my way out of town.' He pushed off the table, and Scott stood up and came over to him.

Before Sumner knew what he was about the vet leaned in and hugged him, surprising Sumner.

'I just had to do that. I never thought I'd meet up with anyone that knew Rachel.' His voice broke at the end.

Sumner touched his shoulder. 'This meeting will always be important to me.'

'Try not to get yourself killed out there.'

'That will be my second-most important goal,' Sumner assured him.

At the jail, Sumner sat his mount for a long moment, still thinking of Scott with his aunt. Before all that trouble violently aborted her life. In Sumner's head, those killers were all mixed up with Pritchard and Guthrie, and their faces often swam around and switched identities before sliding into a dark place reserved for dark thoughts.

When he entered the white-washed building, he found himself in a room with a battered old desk to his right and a middle-aged man sitting behind it, studying some wanted dodgers. On the left was a pot-belly stove and a poster board on the wall where a few posters were tacked up. The marshal, a man named Uriah Tate, looked up distractedly when Sumner came in.

'What can I do for you, mister?' he asked, taking in Sumner's gunslinger look.

'I'm looking for a couple of men,' Sumner said. 'I was hoping you could help me.'

Tate scowled slightly at him. 'Looking for men? What for?'

Sumner sighed. 'I have business with them.'

Tate rose from his chair and came around the desk. He was soft-looking, with a bulging middle and a lined face. 'Who are these men, mister?'

'They're wanted by the U.S. Marshal in Fort Sill. For various crimes.'

Tate sat on the edge of his desk. 'I see. And you've been deputized?'

'Something like that.'

Tate looked at Sumner's Colt. 'So you intend to arrest them?'

'Something like that.'

Tate grinned. 'You're a man of a few words. Are these

two men a couple of weasels named Guthrie and Pritchard?'

'That's them.'

'You missed them by a few days. They stayed at the local hotel just one night. Drank heavy at the Prairie Schooner down the street. Asked Luke Mallory for a job there. Said he needed protection from the reformers, like what's going on in Dodge. Mallory said we haven't had any reformers here yet, and sent them on their way. He didn't like their looks. That night somebody threw a brick through the Schooner's front window and then shot up the interior. My deputy was sound asleep here and didn't hear a thing. Then next morning the two men were gone.'

'Sounds like them,' Sumner muttered.

Tate met Sumner's eye. 'Is there something personal going on between you and them two?'

Sumner held his look. 'Yes.'

Tate nodded. 'All right. I won't inquire further. But it looks like you got your work cut out for you.'

'I know that.'

'Frankly, I think we was lucky with them. If they had stayed around to raise hell, I might not have been able to do much of anything about it. I ain't no gunslinger. When I first pinned this badge on a few years back, a couple like them rode in. It was one of them hard-winter February days when it was so cold your spit would freeze before it hit the ground. I remember they wore thick sheepskin coats and ear-flap hats. They robbed two saloons and a store, then murdered the storekeeper and raped his wife. When I went to arrest them, they had ridden out. I was never so secretly relieved in my life.'

'And your point is?'

'There's enough trouble that will come at you eventually, without you going looking for it.'

'I didn't go looking,' Sumner said. 'This trouble found me. I'm just still in the middle of it.'

Tate nodded. 'Listen.'

'Yes?'

'If you're still around when it's over, I need a real deputy here. And I think you would fill the bill.'

Sumner smiled at him. 'I'll remember that.'

'A good man is as hard to find nowadays as a banker in heaven. And I can tell when I see one.'

'You don't know my past,' Sumner reminded him.

'It don't matter. The man I see in front of me now is the one that counts.'

'Well, I doubt I'd ever pin a badge on. Anyway, if things go right, there's a girl in Texas.'

Tate grinned again. 'Ah. Well, I couldn't compete with that.'

Sumner stuck his hand out and Tate took it and felt the strength in it. 'Keep the peace, Marshal.'

'*Vaya con Dios,*' Tate responded.

Sumner figured the stallion needed rest and some decent food, so he billeted it at a nearby hostelry and stayed a night at the local hotel. The room was small and smelled of tobacco smoke and perfume, but Sumner was too tired to care. He slept well, but dreamt of Corey. He and Corey were looking for work together at a ranch near Blaneyville, and Corey was telling him that Jane would have a nice stew ready for them when they returned. When he woke from that, at three a.m., he thought for a moment he was at the Madison farm. When he realized where he was and what lay ahead for him, a heavy mood overcame him until he fell asleep again.

He rode out of Sulphur Creek just after dawn, knowing he was not likely to ever see the place again. It was almost summer now, and even though each day took him farther north, the days were getting warmer. He stopped more regularly, and drank from the canteen often. At midday he found a tiny stream, a mere rivulet of running water, and let his mount drink its fill.

The terrain was changing with almost every hour. The arid-country flora was gone, replaced with flowering shrubs and tall trees. He rode through vast grasslands and ranches, seeing small bunches of grazing cattle in a grass-grown gullet, chewing their cuds into a soft breeze.

In late afternoon he started to look for a place to camp for the night, since Dodge City was still a half day's ride away. But then he spotted a hunter's cabin crouching in a solitary stand of young cottonwoods.

He reined the black horse in and studied the scene. A light smoke came from a chimney of the cabin, but there were no horses tethered or corraled outside. He touched his spurs to the stallion's flanks and rode up to the cabin. He was low on food, and hoped he might buy some coffee and maybe a couple of corn dodgers from the cabin's owner if he returned.

He dismounted and tethered the horse, then walked over to the door. It was open. 'Anyone here?' he called out.

No response. He cautiously entered the cabin and

looked around. It was a one room affair. Double bunk, table, chairs. A lit fireplace with a coffee pot hanging above it. He found a tin cup beside the fireplace and poured himself a cup of warm coffee, knowing that visitors were entitled to that courtesy, out on the trail. He stood there looking around. Sipping the coffee.

'Maybe I can pick up a tin of something here, too,' he said to himself. But he didn't want to wait long for the owner. He wanted to make some more miles before the day was over.

He finally threw the remains of his coffee into the fire, and it sizzled there. He was about to leave when he heard the sound of hoof beats, and there were two horses.

He walked to the door just as two rough-looking men dismounted. One of them, a middle-aged fellow with a stoop, had pulled an American eight-gauge shotgun from its saddle scabbard and it was already aimed at Sumner. The other man, younger and wiry, had drawn a Winchester rifle.

'What the hell do you think you're doing, mister?' the older man growled at Sumner. The two looked like brothers.

Sumner sighed. 'I saw your cabin and helped myself to a cup of your coffee,' he said easily. 'I was waiting for you to get back, hoping you could sell me some for the trail.'

'You stole our coffee?' the younger one said fiercely. He had rheumy, blank-looking eyes and spoke in a high, reedy voice.

'Shut up, Lenny,' his older brother barked out.

Lenny gave him a blistering look. 'I saw him first! You can't take what's mine, Eben!'

The elder brother stepped forward and looked

113

Sumner over. 'Throw it down, mister.'

'This is getting ridiculous,' Sumner said to himself. 'What?'

'I'm not a thief. I drank a small cup of your coffee. I'll pay you for it if you want it that way. There's no need for this.'

'Maybe you ain't listening,' Eben said in a low voice.

The dangerous shotgun was aimed at Sumner's midsection. And, unlike the fake Bible drummer, he had kept his distance, and wanted the revolver thrown to the ground.

Sumner hesitated. He could draw and get a shot in. But if that American went off, it would tear him in half. And then there was the obviously backward brother, hoping for a chance to use the Winchester.

Sumner reluctantly drew the Peacemaker and threw it to the ground. He was wearing his tong coat jacket, and it felt very hot on him now.

'All right, I'm disarmed. Now will you hear me out?'

The fellow called Eben picked the Colt up and turned it over in his hand. Brushed it off. 'Nice balance.' He stuffed it into his belt. 'I reckon the Rikers sent you.'

'What?' Sumner asked impatiently.

'Are there more coming?'

'I don't know what the hell you're talking about. I'm on my way to Dodge. I have important business there and I'd like to be on my way.'

'He'd like to be on his way!' Lenny cackled. 'You hear that, Eben? This boy thinks he's going somewhere!'

'I heard,' Eben responded. 'Take it easy, boy.'

'You said I could have the next one,' Lenny pleaded. 'Don't go back on your word, Eben.'

This is different,' Eben said, still looking Sumner over. 'This boy come here after us. Because of what we done to that Riker boy.'

'I've never heard of the Rikers,' Sumner said rather loudly. Inside, something had coiled tight. 'Look, I've got money I can give you. You can have it all. Just let me go on my way. I have to get to Dodge City.'

'If we want your money, we'll take it,' Eben said coolly. 'Now, you just turn yourself around and get right back in that cabin, mister.'

'Now, wait—'

Lenny stepped forward and leveled the Winchester at Sumner's face. 'He's just asking for it, ain't he, Eben? Can I?'

'You better get your butt inside, mister,' Eben told him. 'While I still got control of this excited brother of mine.'

Sumner took another look at breathing-hard Lenny, and at the rifle aimed at his belly, and with a heavy sigh, turned and went into the cabin again. The other two right behind him.

'Hold it right there,' Eben's voice came to him. He was in the center of the room, beside the old table. 'Now turn around.'

Sumner turned and saw that Eben had stationed himself against the front door, which he had closed. He had never taken the shotgun off Sumner.

'Go get that rope over in the corner there,' he directed Lenny. 'And cut a couple feet off the end. Then bring it over here and tie his hands up.'

Lenny holstered the rifle and followed his brother's orders eagerly, scurrying about on what appeared to be a

115

deformed left leg. There was only one gun on Sumner now, but Eben was watching him like a hawk with that big gun. Sumner knew that if he made the slightest move, he would have a hole in him you could stuff your fist through.

Lenny came over to Sumner with the rope, facing him with an unnerving grin.

'Not in front, you fool!' Eben growled at him. 'Tie them in back!'

Lenny limped around Sumner and tied his hands back there. Sumner tried with modest success to keep his hands slightly apart while the rope was being secured.

'You should've took the coat off,' Eben complained. 'But never mind now. You can go get that billy we keep in the box.'

Lenny left him again, and Sumner began to worry about what they might have in mind. But at least they had made a small first mistake. If they had removed his black jacket, they would have discovered the Harrington Derringer at the small of his back, in its special, thin cut-down holster.

When Lenny returned, he was carrying a billy club used by town marshals to subdue drunks. It was ten inches long and made of oak, with a leather loop at its handle end. Lenny stood before him, smacking it into his other hand.

'Now, Eben?'

'No, not yet,' Eben told him. 'Set yourself on that chair, Riker.'

Sumner followed his command, seating himself on a rickety straight chair near the table. 'My name is Sumner,' he said heavily. 'And I have nothing to tell you about the Rikers. I just rode up here from the Territory. I'm looking for two US Deputy Marshals.'

Eben squinted down on him. 'Better tie his ankles up, too,' he said in a thoughtful tone.

In just moments, Lenny had cut another length of rope and bound Sumner's feet together. Now he was almost helpless.

Eben came over and laid the shotgun on the table. There were no guns on Sumner now, but both men were armed on their gun-belts. Eben's sidearm was a Joslyn .44, which was an accurate gun. He came over to Sumner, unafraid of him now.

'Are you an older brother? To the boy we dealt with here?'

'Are you hard of hearing?' Sumner said darkly. 'My name is Sumner. I'm originally from Texas. I've never met a Riker in my life. When did you – when was this other Riker here? How long ago?'

'You know the answer to that,' Eben said.

'He's funning with us, Eben!' Lenny shouted wildly.

'You don't level with us, Lenny will commence on you,' Eben told Sumner, leaning toward him.

'Humor me before you turn him loose,' Sumner said heavily. 'When was the Riker boy here?'

Eben shrugged. 'A couple years back. But we heard from you boys since then.'

'I was in Texas State Prison two years ago. Then I was working for Clay Allison. You can check. I couldn't have known anything about Riker, or what you did to him.'

Eben nodded to his brother and suddenly the billy club came at Sumner's head. It struck him on the left side of his head and face, fracturing the cheek bone under Sumner's eye. Raw pain rocketed through Sumner's head, and a dark chasm welled in on him. He saw a movement where Lenny's arm was being raised again, and heard Eben's voice as if through a long tunnel.

'No. That's enough for now.'

Sumner almost fell off the chair. Sharp daggers of pain stabbed at him under his left eye, where his eye was swelling shut fast. He didn't quite lose consciousness, but was breathing raggedly.

'You . . . sonsofbitches.'

'Did you hear what he called us, Bubba?'

But Eben was ignoring Lenny. He came and sat down on a second chair, facing Sumner. 'He's still with us. Listen, stranger. Maybe I believe you. Anyway, we'll just hope you're the last of them. But it's kind of unlucky for you. That you come past here. 'Cause Lenny's ready for some entertainment again. And I don't like to deprive him too long. He could turn on me, you see.'

Sumner was coming around, and he now stared hard at Eben, and then at the psychopath grinning at him. What the hell have I fallen into, he asked himself. Now it looked like all his plans were aborted, and Corey's death would go unanswered. All because he stopped at this loony bin.

He couldn't let that happen. It would be an indescribable abomination. He had to do something. But he was helpless. In their power.

'If you'll let me go,' he gasped out, 'I can get you more money than I have with me. I can promise you that.'

'We never really needed money,' Eben assured him. 'We just get along by ourselves And I just have to give

118

Lenny his way sometimes. To keep him calm, you know.'

'Oh God,' Sumner mumbled.

'Can I use the iron, Eben?' Sumner heard the younger brother ask.

'Oh, all right. But don't make it last forever. I'll be getting hungry pretty soon here.'

Sumner saw Lenny scurry over to the fireplace, and throw a couple of logs onto the fire, making it crackle and flare up. Then he took an iron rod used for stirring up the fire, and laid an end of it on the flames. He turned and flashed a twisted grin at Sumner.

'It will be ready for you directly,' his reedy voice announced.

It was clear to Sumner now what they had planned for him. Eben was going to let his deranged brother murder Sumner. In a most unpleasant way. Which was undoubtedly what had happened to that Riker they talked about. Eben was busy now getting some canned goods down from a shelf. Lenny hovered over Sumner, grinning psychotically. He had found a sharp-pointed table knife and now held it up to Sumner's right eye, an inch or two away.

'I could give this a shove, and you couldn't see what's going to happen,' he said.

Sumner held his breath. One jab from that knife and he would be half-blind. Two jabs and his life was substantially over, whatever else occurred.

'I'd rather see it happen,' he managed.

'Good,' Lenny hissed. 'Better for me.' He left Sumner and returned to the fireplace.

Sumner had begun working at the rope that held his hands, with little result. The effort, also, was causing the rope to cut into his flesh, and his wrists were already hurting from the trauma. As he worked at it, though, he felt a sharp sliver of wood protruding slightly from an upright that formed the back of the chair. While Lenny was engaged at the fire, Sumner manipulated the knot in the rope so it caught on the sliver, and when he pushed downward, the sliver caught the knot and pulled at it.

He had to be careful. When Lenny was at the fire, he had a view of Sumner's back from the right side. Sumner worked the knot.

'Don't take it out of there till it's good and hot,' Eben said from across the room. 'I want to get this over with.'

'All right, Eben,' Lenny responded. He came over to Sumner, and Sumner stopped working the knot. Lenny came around to face him again.

'The end of that poker will be red hot, Riker. Do you know what that does to a man's flesh?' A wild look.

Sumner carefully resumed working the knot. He felt it loosening slightly. But he couldn't make a movement that could be seen from Lenny's viewpoint.

'I asked you a question, Riker. You want it in the face first? I think the belly is a soft spot o start.' He leaned forward and ripped Sumner's shirt open, making buttons fly across he room. Sumner flinched but said nothing. The knot was loose now, and he reached out with a finger and began pulling the rope free.

Lenny returned to the fire just as Eben spoke to him. 'Get on with that. I'm going outside in a minute to look in his saddle bags. I want it over when I get back in here.'

'All right, Eben,' Lenny grunted.

Eben exited the cabin then, and Sumner realized they had made their second mistake. Now Lenny came back from the fire, and he was holding the iron poker that glowed red at its end. Lenny held the other end with a gloved hand.

'Now,' he was saying. 'The fun begins. This is like a party, ain't it?'

Behind his back, the rope fell off Sumner's wrists. 'I like parties,' Sumner said quietly. 'But it looks like your brother is in trouble out there.'

Lenny frowned. 'Huh?' He turned just for a moment to peer through the open doorway.

In that moment, Sumner pulled his jacket up in back, grabbed the Derringer with his bloody right hand, and brought it around to level on Lenny just as he turned back to Sumner.

'Surprise!' Sumner growled out. Then the one-shot Derringer barked out in the room and blew a small hole in Lenny's lower face, just beside his nose.

The lead traveled through Lenny's brain and blew bone and matter out of the back of his skull. His head whiplashed, a deep frown taking over his face. Then he toppled to the floor at Sumner's feet, the hot poker lying on his chest and slowly burning a hole in it.

Sumner heard Eben yell, 'What the hell!' from out in the encroaching dusk, then he came running back to the cabin, gun drawn.

Sumner, though, seeing the American shotgun still on the kitchen table, grabbed it from his sitting position, turned its muzzle toward the door, and squeezed one of its triggers just as Eben came back in. The shotgun blasted its thunder into the close confines of the cabin, and Eben was struck at waist level, the shot almost tearing him in half. He went flying back out of the cabin

121

as his revolver went off once and tore a chunk out of the overhead rafters behind Sumner.

Sumner rose from the chair. His wrists were bleeding and his left eye was almost swollen closed. There were still sharp stabbing pains from the busted cheek bone. But, miraculously, he was alive.

He walked around the table and looked down at Lenny's lifeless body with the poker smouldering on it. He savagely kicked the corpse in the side. Then he walked outside the door and examined Eben.

The older brother, the man who criminally gave his psychotic sibling the licence to kill savagely, lay with his torso in one direction and his legs in another. There was almost nothing in between but shredded flesh. He lay in a widening pool of blood.

Sumner saw double for a moment, then his focus returned. 'That's for all those others, you soulless sonofabitch!' he spat out.

He went back inside, and smelled the odor of burnt flesh where Lenny's chest was vulnerable to the poker. Sumner picked the poker up and hurled it into the fireplace, where the fire angrily reacted.

Sumner stepped over the body of his tormenter and went over to a shelf on the wall, where Eben had deposited his Colt, and retrieved and holstered it. Then he found a pot of stew sitting near the fireplace. He heated it up, found a spoon, and sat down at the table and ate a meal there, ignoring the corpses littering the area.

When he was finally finished, he left the cabin and quieted the stallion, which was still waiting patiently for his return, but seemed skitterish. He boarded it painfully. Thinking that this was beginning to look more like an odyssey than a mission.

'Well,' he said to his mount. 'Our goal is still the same. And we should still be in Dodge City tomorrow. Let's find us a good place to rest tonight.'

He figured he would need it.

CHAPTER SEVEN

Sumner found a campsite in a small grove of trees a couple of hours after he left the cabin, and spent a restless night with his left eye waking him regularly. There was no water for the stallion, and Sumner drank what was left in his canteen. When dawn broke across the eastern horizon with pastel brush strokes of lavender and crimson, Sumner felt as if he hadn't slept at all. His eye and cheek, though, had quit attacking him with sharp needles of pain and the swelling in his eye had subsided. Blood had caked on his wrists and he had found a second shirt in his saddle-bags to replace the torn one. By the time he rode out, he was feeling just a little better, and still very grateful to be alive. When he first awoke, he had had the strongest urge to return to the cabin and kick Lenny's corpse a last time.

It was just a few hours' ride to Dodge City, and Sumner arrived there in early afternoon. Riding along the main street, Sumner was impressed by the lively look of the town, a mood that belied the trouble the city was experiencing now. Carriages and buggies rolled along the broad street, and stores were busy with customers. He passed a saloon called the Long Branch and a couple smaller ones on his way through town, and found the city marshal's office in a weathered building at the end of the street. He stopped the tired stallion just in front of the entrance and situated it at a hitching post.

'You'll get a rest now,' he told it. 'I'll get you bedded down shortly.'

When he entered the place, there was nobody in sight. He was in a cluttered room, with papers piled on an old desk and boxes stacked in a corner. There were two poster boards on a back wall, with wanted posters and others that looked as if they had been there for years. A corridor led from the room to holding cells at the rear of the building. Sumner walked down the corridor to the cells and found a bulky-looking man there taking a mattress off a cot in one of the cells. The fellow looked up when he heard Sumner approach.

'Afternoon,' Sumner greeted him.

The other man came out of the cell and looked Sumner over with a wary stare.

'You another of them hired guns that Luke Short brought in?' He wore a badge prominently on his vest.

'I don't know Luke Short,' Sumner said.

'Hmmph.' He studied Sumner's face. It was black and blue around his left eye and on his cheek. 'Did you run into a post or something?'

'My horse kicked me,' Sumner said.

'I'd get me another horse,' was the response. 'I'm Marshal Hartman. You ought to have that looked at.'

'It will heal,' Sumner said. 'You think we could talk for a minute, Marshal?'

L.C. Hartman nodded. 'Come on up front. I got

coffee on if you want some.'

'I'll pass.'

They went back to the office and sat at Hartman's desk. Hartman poured himself a cup of coffee. 'Now. How can I help you, young man?'

'I'm looking for a couple of fugitives, and thought you might be able to help me with it.'

'Oh. You're one of them.' With disdain.

'I'm not looking for bounties. It's personal.'

'Well. Who are these men?'

Sumner told him about the twosome, and Hartman listened carefully. 'As it turns out, I just got posters on them two. From Fort Sill. They both got bounties on their heads. I ain't seen either of them, but I hear a gun-fighter-type rode in here a few days ago. He was alone.'

'Did you hear what he looked like?'

'Not really. I think he tried to hire on for Luke Short.'

Sumner frowned. 'Who is this Luke Short?'

Hartman settled back on his chair. 'You obviously ain't from Kansas, boy. You landed yourself right in the middle of what they're calling the Dodge City War. The reformers moved in here lock, stock and barrel some months ago. To close down the saloons in accordance with state law. And rid the town of prostitutes. And they expected me to do their dirty work. Well, I got rid of the saloon girls. But if I closed them saloons down, I'd have a cowboy riot on my hands.'

'Sounds like quite a mess,' Sumner offered.

'That ain't the half of it. In the middle of all that, I tried to arrest Luke Short. He owns the Long Branch. And he actually drew down on me. We both fired, and he got a nick on his arm. Me and my deputy sent him packing then, as an alternative to a jail term. But a month ago he was back here with two gunfighters and reopened the saloon. He says I broke the law by going against him. That Mayor Webster won't lift a finger to help. The gunmen Short brought back with him are Wyatt Earp and Bat Masterson.'

'But they're both lawmen themselves.'

'They say they're just here to keep the peace. A couple of the reformers have vowed to burn the saloons to the ground.'

'Didn't Earp wear a badge here once?'

Hartman nodded. 'He cleaned this town up almost single-handed. The mayor thinks he's a damn hero. Of course, that was a few years back. Since the reformers heard of his return, they've vowed to hire their own guns. Somebody is going to get killed here right soon, you can count on it. And this fellow you're after, if he's here, might be the first one to pull the trigger.'

Sumner sat there thinking. He touched his hand to the black, bruised place on his face. 'I guess my first stop would be the Long Branch Saloon.'

Hartman glanced at the Peacemaker on Sumner's hip. He had discarded the coat again now, and was wearing just the vest over his clean shirt.

'Are you good with that thing?'

Sumner grunted out a laugh. 'Oh, I know where to oil it.'

'Luke Short may try to hire you,' Hartman told him. 'I think he intends to build a small army over there.'

Sumner rose from his chair. 'Thanks for the sit down, Marshal. I might stop back in. Depending on how things go.'

Hartman rose, too. He liked the looks of Sumner, despite his rough appearance. 'Good luck to you, mister.'

'The name is Sumner.'

Hartman frowned at him. 'The boy that killed Curly Quentin?'

Sumner sighed. 'I guess I won't ever get past that.'

'I'll be damned!' Hartman took another look at the Colt.

'I'll be on my way, Marshal.'

'I wasn't going to mention this. But the money on the heads of them two deputies you're looking for is pretty big.'

'That's not my business,' Sumner said. 'You keep safe now, Marshal.'

'Son, that gets tougher by the day.'

Sumner found the local hostelry after he left the marshal, and got his mount bedded down and fed. Then he went to a small hotel near the Long Branch Saloon and checked in, just in case he would need to spend the night. He had a light meal in the hotel dining room, and then walked across the street to the saloon.

It was early, and there were just a few patrons present, town men sitting and drinking quietly. Sumner sat down at a table near the door, and looked around. He found it interesting that the newcomer to town was alone. But he spotted neither Pritchard nor Guthrie in the place at that moment.

A bartender came out to him and asked for his order and Sumner requested a bottle of Red Top Rye and a glass.

'Yes, sir. Can I interest you in a couple of boiled eggs and a hot biscuit?'

'No, thanks. Listen, have you had any strangers in looking for work here?'

'Oh, I wouldn't know. You'd have to ask Mr Short.'

'Is he available?'

'I'll go get him when I get your rye.'

He returned a moment later and deposited the bottle on Sumner's table, and two shot glasses. 'In case you have company. Mr Short is coming.'

It was just a moment later when Sumner was pouring himself a drink that Luke Short approached Sumner's table with another man. Luke was tall and good-looking, wearing a fancy brocaded vest, and Sumner correctly picked him out from his companion. The other man was dressed in a black suit and black lariat tie and wore a short handlebar moustache. He looked more like an accountant than a gunman. But he also looked very physical.

'Evening, stranger,' Luke said, standing at the table now. 'I'm the owner here. My name is Luke Short, and this handsome fellow beside me is Wyatt Earp.'

Sumner rose from his chair. 'Mr Earp. Your reputation precedes you.'

Wyatt was staring at Sumner's black eye. He wore a Peacemaker just like the one on Sumner's belt. 'Have you been brawling in one of our saloons, boy?'

'My mount kicked me. Glad to meet you, Mr Short. I'm Wesley Sumner.'

The two exchanged a look. 'Curly Quentin,' Luke said to Wyatt.

Wyatt nodded. 'And knew Clay Allison, I hear.'

'I worked for him on his ranch for a while,' Sumner admitted.

'A damn good man with a gun,' Wyatt said. 'But if he'd shown up in Tombstone, I'd have had to arrest him.'

Sumner gave him a rare grin. 'Will you sit with me for a drink?'

The two seated themselves at the table with him, and Sumner ordered a third glass and the bartender brought it. Sumner poured them all a drink.

'To our mutual health,' Sumner toasted, raising his glass.

They both knew what he meant. They swigged the rye.

'I understand you're looking for work,' Luke Short said then.

'No, no,' Sumner said. 'I was looking for a man that might have asked for work here.'

'Why do you want him?' Wyatt asked bluntly.

Sumner looked over at him. Earp was a presence at the table. He gave off an aura of authority. When he spoke, people listened. Sumner hesitated. 'It's a personal grievance,' he finally said.

Wyatt laughed in his throat. 'Sounds like the story of my life. In Tombstone.'

'I heard something about that,' Sumner said.

'Wyatt's brother Morgan was killed,' Luke said. 'So Wyatt took his badge off, rode out after the three shooters, and killed every last one of the murdering bastards.'

'I turned lawless again,' Wyatt offered, remembering. 'I had a whole damn sheriff's posse after me while it was happening.'

Sumner smiled. He was beginning to like this big reputation lawman. 'You said "Again".'

'Oh, Wyatt was pretty wild as a youngster,' Luke explained.

'Didn't you spend a spell in prison, Sumner?' Wyatt asked curiously.

Sumner took a deep breath in. 'A while, yes.'

'You sound a lot like me, kid.' Wyatt grinned.

Sumner met Wyatt's eye. That was the biggest compliment he had ever received. 'That honors me, Wyatt.'

'Nonsense. Look, who is this man you're looking for?'

'There are actually two men,' Sumner said. 'But one of them might have ridden in here recently.'

'Big man, with a scar on his face?' Luke asked.

Sumner nodded. 'That sounds like Pritchard.'

'Yes, that's the name he gave,' Wyatt said.

'He asked me for a job,' Luke added. 'But I didn't like the way he looked. Or acted. I turned him down. Oh, he said something to himself then. He said he should have gone to Cimarron with another man. I can't remember the name.'

'Was it Guthrie?'

'That was it. I got the idea they had had a falling out and went separate ways. Pritchard said he would try down the street, so he might have been hired by one of the other saloons. They're afraid of the reformers.'

'I'll check it out,' Sumner said.

'You look like a man that can handle himself,' Wyatt said, looking him over again. 'Luke here could probably put you on right here at the Long Branch. You could join Masterson and me to keep a watch over this place. Our city marshal doesn't have the gunpower to do it.'

Sumner shook his head. 'I'm not looking for a job, gentlemen. But I appreciate the offer.'

'You're kind of single-minded right now.' Wyatt smiled.

131

Sumner nodded. 'That's it.'

'The same way I was in Tombstone,' Wyatt recalled. 'Did these boys kill somebody you knew?'

'They did. And they did it under the color of the law. They were federal marshals.'

'Over in the Territory?'

Sumner nodded.

'Those boys are the worst,' Wyatt told him. 'They hire just anybody that applies over there. Because they're always so short-handed. If this Pritchard is here, would you need some help with him?'

Sumner was impressed. He was being offered help by the most feared gunfighter and ex-lawman of the southwest. 'Like I said, Wyatt. This is personal. But thanks.'

'You're turning down some big help there, boy,' Luke said.

'You don't have to tell me that.' He downed a second drink. 'Well. The bottle is yours, gentlemen. I have some looking to do.'

'Why don't you ask at that hotel across the street?' Luke suggested. 'I think I saw Pritchard walk over there.'

'Good idea. Thanks.' He rose.

'Listen, Sumner.' From Wyatt Earp.

'Yes?' Sumner replied.

'When you go after a man with fire in your belly, be careful. Stoke the fire fast. It can hamper your efficiency.'

Again, Sumner was impressed. 'I'll remember that, Wyatt.'

Then he left them staring after him.

At the hotel across the street, where he had registered himself earlier, Sumner spoke to the same desk clerk who had registered him.

'Would you like your room key, sir?'

'No. I just heard that a friend of mine might also be registered here. Do you have a man named Duke Pritchard here?'

'Why, yes, we do. I could send you up to his room, but he isn't there now.'

'Would you know where I can find him?'

'He met up with a couple of other men that work where he does. I think he might have rode out to a cabin one of them owns. I heard him mention it.' He pushed a pair of rimless spectacles up farther on his bony nose.

'Where would that be?' Sumner asked him.

'I have no idea. But I think all of them work at the same place.'

Sumner frowned at him. 'Well?'

'Oh. They work at that saloon near the bank. It's called the Lost Heifer. He would be there most any night. He's a kind of security guard there. To throw out any of them reform people that might wander in.'

Sumner nodded. He paused, then took some coins from a pocket and laid them on the counter between them. 'Here. For keeping the room open for me. In case I can't use it tonight.'

The clerk eyed him curiously. 'Aren't you staying?'

'I can't say for sure right now. But maybe I will take that key after all. When do you serve the evening meal?'

'That will be ready at six.'

Sumner thanked him and went up a flight of stairs to his small, spartan room with its iron bed and one straight chair in a corner. There was a sign hanging over the bed that announced *House Rules* and listed half a dozen.

Sumner flopped down tiredly on the lumpy bed and

slept for three hours without waking up or even moving. He had had no idea how tired he had become. When he went across the hall to a bathroom to wash up, he found that the color around his eye and cheek was turning a light lavender, and yellow. It felt much better and he knew the break there would soon heal.

He had gotten the room number of Pritchard from the clerk, but when he stopped near it there was no sound coming from inside and he rightfully surmised that Pritchard was not there. He went on downstairs to eat his evening meal, and ate it leisurely, with a tension slowly building inside him. He remembered Wyatt Earp's advice to him, and made a conscious effort to push the emotion back. He wondered if Pritchard would show up at the small dining room, but he didn't.

At a quarter to eight he left the hotel and walked down to the Lost Heifer Saloon. It was dusk outside and lamps were already lit in the saloon. When he entered, he saw that there was just a small crowd there, drinking and talking quietly at several tables. He stopped just inside the doors and looked around.

At the center of the room, sitting at a table with two other men, was Duke Pritchard.

Sumner's eyes narrowed down to a deadly-looking scowl. This was it.

The end of a very long trail.

Pritchard was laughing and joking with his comrades and seemed to be having a good time.

Then he spotted Sumner standing just inside the doors.

His hard eyes narrowed, and the two men sitting with him fell silent, following his stare. 'What the hell!'

Pritchard muttered.

'What is it?' the tall, rawboned man on his right asked.

The second one was just staring sober-faced at Sumner.

Sumner felt something harden inside him. Memories flew through his head like birds of prey, ripping at Sumner's psyche. Pritchard beating on Corey with that wicked club until Corey was senseless. He fought to keep the thing under control that was boiling at his gut. He moved a few paces toward the table, and stopped again.

'Pritchard,' he uttered in a deadly tone.

Pritchard squinted at him. 'The kid from Fort Sill?' He had no trepidation about Sumner's presence. He remembered him as an awkward young man who didn't even wear a gun.

'The same,' Sumner growled. 'Corey Madison's friend.'

Pritchard grinned and shook his head. 'I remember you two now. Gabriel hanged your little friend, didn't he?'

'He never made it to the gallows,' Sumner said. 'You beat him to death.'

Suddenly all noise in the saloon had ceased. All eyes were now on the Pritchard table, and on Sumner.

'Can I help it if he was a weak little bastard?' Pritchard laughed. He glanced at the Colt on Sumner's hip. 'I see you finally decided to strap a gun on. Have you fired it yet? I reckon you'll get the hang of it after a while, kid. When you learn where the trigger is.'

Pritchard laughed again, more loudly, and the slim man joined in. The third gunman, also a saloon hire, was still appraising Sumner carefully.

'Hell, I'll let bygones be bygones,' Pritchard added then. 'In fact, you can have a drink with us. If you're old enough.'

More laughter. But only at Pritchard's table. An almost palpable tension had crowded into the room and taken the breath away from many patrons.

'You have to pay for Corey,' Sumner said after a moment. He hadn't moved from the place he stopped at, fifteen feet away. There was nothing in his line of fire.

Pritchard screwed his face up. 'Good Jesus! Is that why you come all the way up here? To call me out?' A slow grin. He still had no concern at all about Sumner's presence. 'Boy, do you know how good I am with a gun?'

'I know your exaggerated opinion of yourself,' Sumner said evenly.

Three men at a table behind Pritchard rose carefully and moved over to the bar. A fat bartender looked toward a back room. 'Mr Cates! We might have trouble in here!'

Pritchard had been irritated by Sumner's last remark. He answered the fat man. 'Trouble? Why, this suckling won't be no trouble, Gus. I already took the measure of him back in the Territory.' He glared now at Sumner. 'Why don't you just take your butt out of here, Sumner, while you still can?'

The third man at the table, the one who had remained quiet through the exchange, looked over at Pritchard quickly. 'Did you say Sumner?'

Pritchard returned the look. 'So what?'

The man turned to Sumner. 'Is that Wesley Sumner?'

Sumner was tired of talking. 'Defend yourself, Pritchard.'

The one who had just addressed him, a bulky fellow, rose quickly from his chair. 'Wait! I don't want no part in this! This boy cut down Curly Quentin. He rode with Clay Allison!'

There was a hushed murmuring across the room. Pritchard's ugly face went straight-lined. The fellow speaking settled a Stetson on his head. 'See you later, boys. I got more healthy things to attend to.' And he hurried past Sumner from the saloon. The lanky man still sitting with Pritchard shrugged. 'We don't need him, Duke. Just say the word.' He considered himself fast with his Colt Navy.

'Why don't you take this outside, boys?' From the bartender.

Pritchard was rising slowly from his seat, frowning heavily. His companion did likewise, and moved slightly away from Pritchard.

'Are you calling me out?' Pritchard growled at Sumner. 'You think Quentin was good? I ain't never been beat, boy. Do you really want to die tonight?'

'That's not in my plans,' Sumner told him quietly. 'Go for your iron.'

Pritchard's face crimsoned, and the scar running through his eye turned pink in the dull light of the saloon. 'You asked for it, boy.'

'Let me take him, Duke,' his companion said thickly. 'I won't break a sweat.'

'You can join in,' Pritchard grated out, grinning now.

'Please, boys!' The bartender's final plea.

In the next moment, both Pritchard and the other gunman went for their guns. Sumner saw the action begin in the first split second. Feeling cool now. In charge.

In seconds, the room erupted with the raucous roaring of their guns. Sumner had decided to go for Pritchard first, because of his importance. Sumner's Peacemaker was out blindingly fast and firing at Pritchard's chest while Pritchard was aiming his Colt at Sumner. Sumner's hot lead struck first by a half second and clubbed Pritchard in center torso, exploding through him close under his heart and blowing blood, bone and matter out through his posterior ribs. Pritchard's shot was jerked off target and ripped along Sumner's ribcage as the other gunman's weapon roared out just before Sumner's hammer-fanned blast, with Sumner in a half-crouch. The shot tore at his neck and collar, grazing him there. But Sumner's second shot hit the other man in the throat and destroyed his windpipe before tearing through his cervical spine.

Pritchard went flying off his feet, abject surprise on his thick face as he crashed over the table behind him and hit the floor so hard that nearby patrons felt it shake under their feet. Pritchard looked like he was trying to get up for a moment and his Colt went off again, smashing a lamp up front. The companion had hit the floor beside their table, his hands at his throat, gagging and gasping for air. Sumner watched as his eyes widened and he took his last strangled breath.

Sumner walked over to Pritchard. A patron standing nearby stumbled out of his way. The saloon was cemetery quiet. Sumner looked down on Pritchard and he was still breathing.

'No, I ain't dead, you little weasel,' he coughed out. 'I'll make it. And then look out.'

Sumner aimed the Colt at his chest and fired a last

time, making a couple of patrons jump. Pritchard twitched once there on his back, and his trousers grew wet at the crotch. Then he was finally lifeless.

Sumner looked around the room at the scared faces. Nobody spoke. Nobody moved. He turned toward the door and started holstering his weapon when he heard a double click behind him, behind the bar.

He whirled around just as the bartender was leveling a double-barreled sawed-off shotgun at his face. Sumner fired first, the lead hitting the fat man in the high chest and punching him back hard against the shelves of bottles, the shotgun blasting loudly now and tearing a hole in the tin ceiling a foot wide. Broken glass and liquor fell onto the bartender as he slipped slowly to the floor back there, and out of sight.

Sumner scanned the room again, to deafening silence. He twirled the Peacemaker twice forward, and then backward into its well-oiled holster. From down the bar, a hushed gasp.

'Jesus and Mary!' Whispered. From an old man at the rear.

Sumner turned and left the deathly quiet room.

CHAPTER EIGHT

When Sumner arrived back on the street, it was dark out there. He just stood for a long moment, looking up at the full moon and unwinding. It had been a long journey, and now most of it was over. Pritchard had always been more important than Guthrie. But it wasn't really over till both men were found and justice visited on them.

He returned to his hotel room and sat on his bed, recalling everything he had experienced since he left Fort Sill that long ago day with a warning to the two deputies. That seemed like a thousand years ago now, in a different world.

He'd been in his room less than an hour when a knocking came at the door. He had been propped up on the headboard of the bed, with his gun-belt hanging on the bedpost. He stood up warily, drew the Colt, and called out.

'Who is it?'

A muffled response. 'It's Douglas and Spencer. From the National Prohibition Council.'

Sumner furrowed his brow. He walked to the door

with the Colt hanging from his grasp, at his side. When he opened the door, two men were standing there. Douglas and Spencer. They were both about the same height and build, with round faces and thick middles. The one called Douglas wore spectacles, and he spoke first.

'I'm Jeff Douglas, and this friend here is Owen Spencer. I gather we're speaking to Wesley Sumner?'

Sumner nodded. 'You're from that reform group that's been making all the trouble here in Dodge?'

They exchanged a look. 'The real troublemakers are those who refuse to obey state law,' Spencer offered.

'Do you think we might have a moment of your time, Mr Sumner?' Douglas asked.

Sumner let a slow breath out. It had been a big day and he didn't need this. 'I can spare a minute,' he said reluctantly.

They followed him into the room, holding hats in their hands. Sumner walked over and re-holstered the Peacemaker and they watched his actions carefully. Sumner leaned against the wall beside the bed.

'OK. Make it fast. I'm about to go get something to eat.'

Douglas glanced at Spencer and cleared his throat. 'Well. We just heard what you did at that saloon down the street.'

Sumner grunted. 'News travels fast.'

'It's our understanding that you're not affiliated with any of the saloons. You haven't been hired by them. Is that right?' Douglas pursued.

'Why is that your business?'

Spencer was squinting at Sumner's vest. 'Say, you

know you're bleeding through your vest? On your side there?'

Sumner glanced down at the dark spot. 'Oh. I almost forgot about it.' He touched his hand to his neck on the left side which was burning from the slight graze. It hurt more than the flesh wound along his ribs. 'I'm stopping at the doc's before I eat and get it looked at. Now, if you gentlemen are about finished here, I'm ready to leave.'

'We wondered if you'd be interested in hiring in at the Council,' Douglas blurted out quickly.

'Hiring in?' Sumner frowned.

'As a bodyguard. Like those men at the Long Branch, and the other saloons. They have all the guns, you see. We have a couple of hot-heads who think they can stand up to those people. But they can't. We need someone that could face up to Wyatt Earp. And Masterson.'

Sumner shook his head. 'It would be suicide to stand up to Earp. Even if you got the first shot in.'

The two exchanged another look. 'We heard you could,' Spencer said.

'You heard wrong,' Sumner told them. 'Anyway, I'm not interested in your little war. My advice? Pack up and go back to Kansas City or wherever you came from. All you'll do here is get some people killed. And most of them will be your people.'

'Well, I must say,' Douglas remarked, 'we expected more of you, Sumner.'

'I've disappointed a lot of folks,' Sumner said with a tired smile. 'Now, if you'll excuse me. Your time is up.'

They left somber-faced, with Sumner staring after them shaking his head. He wondered why their kind didn't just stay back in Boston or wherever they hailed from and enjoy what they already had back there.

Sumner stopped very briefly at a local doctor's office when he left the hotel, and got a bandage on his ribs, and had a previous side wound looked at, which was healing nicely. The neck wound required just a bit of salve. After that he had a light meal at a small restaurant not far from the Long Branch, and then walked down to the marshal's office. When he appeared there, L.C. Hartman stared hard at him from his desk.

'I'll be damned! I thought we had trouble before you arrived. But you've managed to turn it up a notch, young man.'

'I gave you fair warning,' Sumner told him. 'Pritchard was a lawless sonofabitch that got what he had coming to him for quite some time.'

'You're a little lawless yourself. I hear you put one in him while he was on his back, and talking.'

'You want to arrest me?'

Hartman shook his head. 'No. I say good riddance. Anyway, I might look foolish if you resisted arrest.'

They both grinned. 'I just wanted to tell you I'm on my way tomorrow early,' Sumner said.

'Off to Cimarron?'

'I'm hoping that's where I'll find him.'

'You're a relentless bastard, ain't you?'

'I know my duty.'

Hartman shuffled some papers on his desk. 'Say, I thought you might want to know this. 'There's $3,000 on Pritchard's head, and $2,000 on Guthrie. Sign this affidavit I got for you here, and I'll put things in motion for you.'

Sumner hadn't even thought about that. He stood

there mulling the idea and found that he felt differently about it now from when he had gunned down Curly Quentin. Maybe Pritchard owed this to him. Maybe Corey would have told him to take it. For Corey. And maybe, eventually, Jane.

Sumner nodded. 'I'll sign it. Can I get them to send it to my Las Animas bank account?'

'That can be done.'

Ten minutes later, Sumner had finished the paperwork and was ready to leave. 'If I don't get a chance to see him again, tell Wyatt Earp I took his advice,' he told Hartman. 'He'll know what I mean.'

Hartman frowned. 'Earp is a hero here. But I wish he'd never rode in. He ain't the law here no more.'

'I think if you just sit back and let it play out, the reformers will settle down and Wyatt will be gone,' Sumner told him. 'In the meantime, play it safe, Marshal.'

'You, too,' Hartman advised him.

After a quiet night back at the hotel, Sumner was on the trail again just after dawn the next morning.

It was a long ride to Cimarron out west of Dodge. It was a sunny, warm day and Sumner arrived in Cimarron mid-afternoon, dusty and tired. The place looked a lot like Dodge, with several saloons lining the main street, and stores and a bank. It was a cow-town, sitting more directly on the cattle drive trails than Dodge City or Wichita, and there were already cowboys standing around outside saloons and stores, or riding their mounts up and down the main thoroughfare.

Sumner had no idea why the two deputies had split up and Guthrie ended up here instead of Dodge. He even had no idea if he would still be here. There was a small hotel near the saloons, and Sumner decided to make that his first stop.

When he stepped into the small reception area, a green-visored clerk was at the desk, behind its counter. Very busy with some papers. He didn't look up when Sumner stood before him.

'Excuse me,' Sumner finally spoke up.

'Yes?' Without looking up.

Sumner frowned, and asked about Guthrie. 'Is he a guest here?'

'We don't talk about our guests. Are you registering?' He finally looked up at Sumner, and stared at the color around Sumner's eye. He looked him up and down haughtily.

'That remains to be seen.'

'Depending on what, sir?'

'On whether Guthrie is registered here.'

The lofty clerk looked exasperated. 'I told you. Information on our guests is private. Now, if you'll excuse me.' He looked back down at his papers.

Sumner walked around the counter and came up to the clerk on its back side.

'Hey! You aren't allowed back here!' the clerk cried out.

Suddenly the Colt was in Sumner's hand as if it had already been there. He stuck the muzzle up against the clerk's long nose.

'Now, are you going to play nice, or am I going to blow your nose for you?'

The clerk's face changed dramatically, the arrogance gone. 'Hey. Take it slow, mister. I never heard of Guthrie.'

'Then why the hell didn't you just say that?' Sumner growled at him. He put the Peacemaker away and left the hotel in a bad mood.

His next stop was a small saloon, where he spoke to a slim bartender. 'He was in here a couple nights ago. I think he prefers the nicer facility up the street there, the Sagebrush.'

'Was he alone?' Sumner asked.

'There was another man, a regular here. Maybe they're cousins, I ain't sure.' He leaned toward Sumner. 'I think they was talking about the bank. You know. But don't quote me on that.'

'That's why he came this way,' Sumner said to himself.

'They're a couple of tough-looking customers,' the barkeep added.

Sumner threw a gold coin on the bar and left without another word.

Outside with his stallion, he knew he should take a room and get a good night's rest. To be fresh, and at his best. But he had come too far and too long to put it off. He took his mount down to the Sagebrush Saloon, tethered it outside, and went in. He didn't recognize Guthrie's horse at the hitching rail out there.

The place was big and rather civilized-looking. A George Catlin painting hung on the wall behind the bar. Potted palms guarded the entrance. Sumner went over to the bar.

'A cold beer,' he said to the bartender. 'And some information.'

The bartender was sweaty from his work. Wisps of hair were combed over a bald head. 'This ain't no information bureau, stranger.'

'This is simple,' Sumner persisted, ignoring the man's rudeness. 'Has a man named Guthrie been in here in the last few days?'

'Never heard of him,' came the grunted response.

But a man behind Sumner, at a nearby table. called out. 'He just left out the back way. He hurried out when he saw you ride up outside.'

Sumner gave the bartender a cold look. He listened for sound out of the back of the building, and heard a horse snicker back there.

'A drifter come in earlier from Dodge. Said somebody called Sumner killed this boy's partner. He thinks you was sent from Fort Sill.'

Sumner heard horse's hoofs out there. 'Cancel that beer order,' he growled at the bartender. Then he hurried out of the front entrance.

When he reached the stallion it had already caught his tension. As he boarded, Guthrie came riding out of a side street about fifty yards away and whipped his mount down the long, hot street, the horse galloping now.

It appeared Guthrie had concluded that Marshal Atkins in Fort Sill had deputized Sumner to find and arrest himself and Pritchard, and the fact that things had gone badly for Pritchard already made him think twice about confronting Sumner.

All that flew through Sumner's head as he now spurred the big horse and headed out of town after Guthrie, to the west.

It was late afternoon, and it was hot. Sumner spurred the stallion and whipped it with the reins. Guthrie was 500 yards ahead, and going at full speed. He was riding a zebra dun mustang pony and it was very fast. In fact,

Sumner lost sight of Guthrie for almost an hour, and then finally saw him again as Guthrie rode into a high outcropping of rocks. Boulders on both sides of the trail. He seemed to slow down as he entered that area, so Sumner did the same as he arrived at the near end of the outcropping.

He was drenched with sweat, and there was foam on the stallion's flanks. A big muscle jumped in its rump, and its mouth was open.

Guthrie was nowhere in sight. Then suddenly a rifle roared out from the rocks up ahead almost 200 yards, just as the stallion reared up in nervousness. Instead of smashing into Sumner's breastbone, the lead struck the horse a grazing shot in its neck.

'Sonofabitch!' Sumner grated out. He slid his Winchester from its saddle scabbard and dismounted quickly as another shot made its thunder and Sumner felt hot lead hit his left arm. He swore again, ducked low, and swatted his mount on its rear from that position, and the horse ran off into the rocks.

Sumner dived for cover behind a boulder. A third shot rang out just as he reached that cover, and sang off the rock above his head.

'You bastard, Guthrie!' Sumner called out. 'This is the end of your dark trail!'

Guthrie's voice called back from behind a high boulder on Sumner's right. 'I guess Atkins sent you to do his dirty work!'

'Atkins didn't send me,' Sumner called back. 'Corey Madison did!'

'Who?'

'The boy you watched Pritchard beat to death!'

Sumner called back. 'Remember that day at Fort Sill when I told you that wasn't the end of it? Well, this is.'

Guthrie laughed loudly. 'Are you crazy? Taking all this on for that snot-nose kid? I didn't touch that little thief. You have no beef with me. Look, I know you tricked Pritchard somehow in a shootout but this is long guns now, boy. Didn't you know I won medals for long shooting? Why do you think I lured you out here? I got you right where I want you.'

'Can you shoot as fast as you talk?' Sumner responded.

'Listen, it could be work killing you. Tell you what. I know the marshal in Cimarron. What if I let you take me in, and I take my chances with the law. You could even claim the bounty. I think it's $1,000.'

'It's $2,000,' Sumner said.

'Better yet! What do you say? This can work out for both of us!'

'I say forget it. You have to pay the bill, Guthrie.'

A brief silence. 'All right, you little Texas rat! I'm going to cut you up into little pieces. There won't be enough left to bury you with when I'm finished with you!'

'Talk is cheap, Guthrie!' But he was concerned about Guthrie's rifle now. Guthrie moved out of cover slightly for a shot, and Sumner fired the Winchester. Up at the rocks, Guthrie yelled and grabbed his right arm.

'You goddamn snake! You're a dead man!' He took aim just as Sumner tried to move to better cover, and hot lead smacked into Sumner's left shoulder. Sumner felt raw pain rocket through him.

He was knocked to the ground and lay on his back, hurting. And at that moment he decided to employ some strategy. He dropped the rifle from his grasp, drew the Peacemaker, and snugged it under his right thigh. Then he lay absolutely motionless.

'What's the matter, Sumner? Can't take a hit?'

No response. The sun burned down on Sumner and sweat inched into his eyes and made them burn. The shot in the high left shoulder was lancing sharp knives of pain through him. A buzzard saw him and circled over-head for a moment, its beady eyes looking for its next meal. A beetle crawled up onto his chest and tried to go under his vest. He remained rock-steady still.

'Sumner?' With curiosity in his voice now.

Sumner had a clear view of Guthrie's cover, and now saw Guthrie warily rise from behind it and tentatively expose himself.

A bluebottle buzzed around Sumner's face. He didn't twitch a muscle. He closed his eyelids so he could just barely see what was before him.

He waited.

In another five minutes, Guthrie came out from the rocks and just stood a long moment. Rifle aimed directly at Sumner's still form.

'Well, I'll be damned,' Sumner heard him say. 'I got you, you goddamn baby rattler!'

Cautiously, Guthrie walked down the slope of ground between him and Sumner.

Sumner lay still.

Guthrie was ten yards away.

Sumner stopped breathing. The beetle was under his vest now. He dismissed it.

Guthrie walked on over to him, and stared down. His face changed.